LET YOUR LIGHT SHINE

LET YOUR LIGHT SHINE

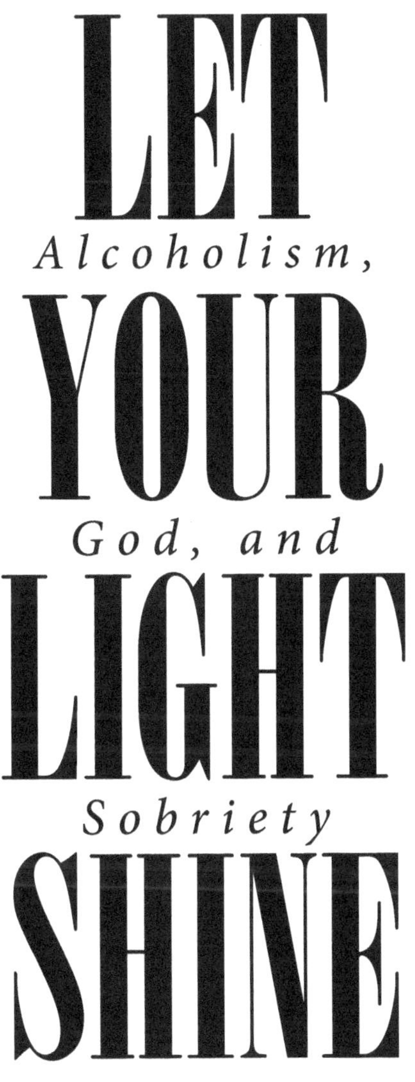

Alcoholism, God, and Sobriety

SANDRA L. BOBBITT

ISBN
978-1-961250-85-7 (Paperback)
978-1-961250-86-4 (eBook)

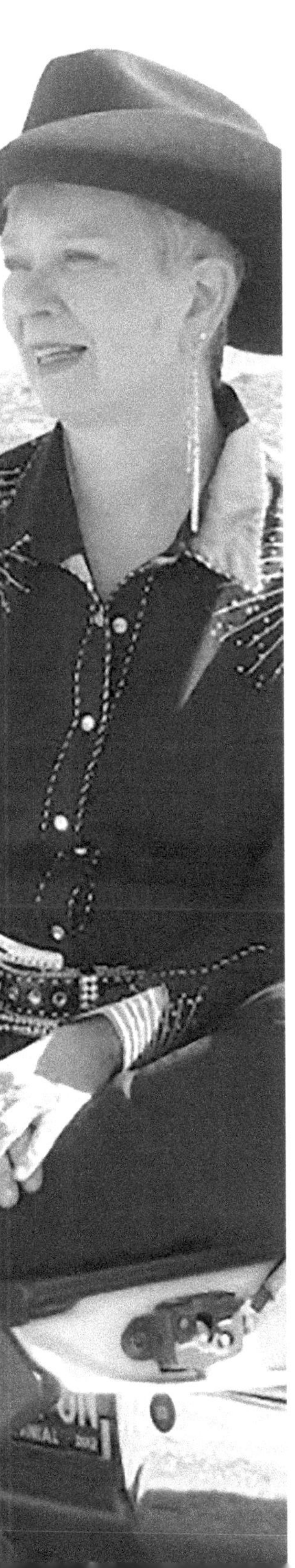

Dedication

This book and its writings are dedicated to those who are fighting the fury of alcohol, whether currently drinking or in rehabilitation and have found sobriety. I invite and encourage alcoholics and recovering alcoholics to read my story. It is a description of loss, abandonment, insecurities, anger, rage, shame, guilt and finally faith. I've found God, recovery, and sobriety after a long career of drinking and now in my journey of rehabilitation.

There is hope for everyone. At one time, I tried to sustain sobriety without professional or spiritual help and failed. Not knowing where to turn or who to seek out, I attempted suicide on two separate occasions. I was fortunate to survive both attempts and it is with my last that I found God, faith, and sobriety.

Sandra L. Bobbitt

TABLE OF CONTENTS

Our gifts are what God gives to us. What
we become is our gift to God.

Sharing our story is one of the greatest
gifts we can give to the world.

A story isn't real until it is told.

We Fell in Love: A Book of Short Stories and Poetry
Life's Little Bumps and Glitches: Poems of Life, Love and Hope
I Had a Dream: Student Nurse to Nurse Practitioner
Love Comes to All of Us: A Book of Short Stories and Poetry
A Heroine's Journey: An Adventure in Self-Reflection
Coming Home: A Road to Healing
Occupational Health and Safety, A Textbook

I WAS A LOST LAMB

I once didn't believe and you stood by me,
I once had no hope and you stood by me,
I once hated my life and you stood by me,
I once tried to die and you stood by me.

I was the one lamb lost in life,
I was the one lamb you gave hope to,
I was the one lamb you brought home.
I was the one lamb you gave life to.

Life is better now that I am home,
Life is better now that I am no longer wandering,
Life is better now that I am a believer,
Life is better now that I am a child of God.

FOREWORD

What sorrow to those who get up early in the morning looking for a drink of alcohol and spend long evenings drinking wine to make themselves flaming drunk. (Isiah5:11)

When I was a young eight-year-old girl, I was introduced to alcohol by my parents. I can remember to this day how the alcohol stung my tongue and how flushed I felt. I liked how the alcohol made me feel and for some unknown reason, I felt grown up. My parents didn't seem to mind that I asked for a sip of their drinks. As I got older, I found ways to sneak alcohol from the liquor cabinet. I would watch my mother in the evenings as she smoked her cigarette and drank her bourbon thinking how sophisticated she looked. Add my handsome dad into the picture and they looked like a typical American couple. Drinking alcohol is what my family did, and I was never denied a drink while growing up.

It was nearly a lifetime before I would admit I was an alcoholic. For years, I knew I had a drinking problem, but I wasn't brave enough to admit to my drinking. It took two attempted overdoses for me to realize that the amount of liquor I was drinking every day would kill me if I continued to drink.

Facts: We can spend a lifetime in therapy discussing our past behaviors without avail. We believe that if we know about the events that had led us to drink, we could cut back on the drinking. When, in fact, all we've done is spend a lot of money on therapy sessions. In

After six decades of drinking, I am sober, and my life has a new meaning.
My story is one of hope and survival, the factors that led me to this
debilitating and lethal disease and how I converted from being an agnostic
to a Christian to find the peace and faith I needed to quit drinking.

My intent when I decided to write my story was to provide a personal
account of my addiction and recovery to render hope to those who have a
desire to quit drinking or quit any mind-altering substance. This is not a
hearts and flowers story. There was little love growing up in my family–
either verbal declarations of love or physical contact of affection. This is the
story of me, an alcoholic living in an alcoholic family where no one talked
about our alcoholism or alcoholic behaviors. We walked around them as
though they didn't exist. Alcoholism plays with the minds of children–
we don't learn to trust, or love. We do, however, learn to be judgmental
and critical. We are scared of life. Social skills aren't known to many of
us until we begin to dig into the reasons we are addicts. Until then, we
learn that isolation– being alone– is a better way to live rather than being
frightened of being around people. These may seem like harsh words, but
they reflect the dysfunctional life of an alcoholic. There is always some
form of emotional and/or physical abuse. For me, it was emotional abuse.

There is light in the darkness for anyone willing to seek it. Along the
journey to sobriety, there are others who have made the journey before us
and are willing to help. Just as we have denied our addiction, we tend to
deny that we need help– yet, all we need to do is ask.

> *For you have spent enough time in the past doing what pagans chose
> to do, live in debauchery, lust, drunkenness, orgies, carousing and
> detestable idolatry. (1 Peter 4:3)*

I was drawn to all the wrong things: I liked to drink, I felt a euphoria when
I drank, and I didn't have a God. I was settled into nothingness; a kind of
nonbeing and I accepted it. I didn't make for a very interesting person; I

was too hard. What I really wanted was only a soft, hazy place to live in, and to be left alone. On the other hand, when I got drunk, I screamed, went crazy, and got out of hand. One kind of behavior didn't fit the other. I didn't care." (Charles Bukowski)

My Prayer

Dear Heavenly Father, give me the courage and fortitude to write an honest and open story of my life of drinking, of the love of God and the faith I've found in my recovery so that it may help those in need.

SERENITY PRAYER

God, give me the serenity to accept the things I cannot change,
The courage to change the things I can,
And the wisdom to know the difference.

CHAPTER ONE

Early Drinking Days

The temptation in your life is no different than what others experience. He will not allow the temptation to be more than you can stand. When you are tempted, He shows you a way out so that you can endure it. (1 Corinthians 1:13)

"My name is Sandy and I'm an alcoholic." I was attending my first Alcoholics Anonymous (AA) meeting at an addiction treatment and rehabilitation program located in the southwest. Anonymity is one of the principles of AA so last names are not used. Each time you wish to speak, you open with this phrase. It's a reminder of your addiction and that everyone in the room is an addict.

As I was sitting in a room with twelve other people, I reflected on how I got to this place in my life and was declaring I was an alcoholic. I had voluntarily admitted myself to a five-day detoxication program, followed by a four-week in-patient alcohol and drug rehabilitation program. This was my first day in rehab and I had not had a drink in six days.

I thought back to my first experience of drinking at the age of eight. I am the eldest of four siblings and during the winter months when we were kids, we came down with an upper respiratory infection at the same time.

Mother would rub Vick's Vapor Rub on our chests, give us a hot toddy and tuck us into bed so we could sweat out the symptoms of whatever ailed us. Mother's hot toddies were laced with bourbon, and I very quickly learned that I liked the taste of alcohol and the warm feeling it gave me. In fact, I would feign being sick for the sole purpose of getting a hot toddy.

Fact: The younger we start drinking, the greater the chance that we will become addicted. A child's environment can certainly contribute to addiction, but the main influence is brain development. The brain of a young person is not fully developed until the age of twenty-one and is therefore more susceptible to the effects of alcohol and drugs.

By the time I was ten years old, my parents allowed me to drink from their alcoholic beverages. They had a lot of adult parties, and it was my job to serve drinks. It's amazing how I was able to sneak some of the mixed concoctions before serving them to their guests.

I grew up in a small rural midwestern town in Kansas and we had one bar–it had a pool table, was smoky and dank. Consequently, mother would drive seven miles to the city where she would visit her choice of bars. One day, not wanting to bar hop alone, she took me with her for company. I was allowed to order an alcoholic drink because I was with a parent. I was fourteen years old.

Fact: Today, alcohol is the most used and abused of all substances, legal and illegal. Alcoholism is now known as Alcohol Use Syndrome (AUD) and is defined as a condition in which a person has a desire or physical need to consume alcohol, even though it has a negative impact on their life.

My mother was an alcoholic and so was my maternal grandfather. I was the only of my three sibling who inherited the tendency for alcoholism. In high school, the only legal alcohol we could get our hands on was 3.2% beer. Liquor wasn't sold on Sunday; however, my mother solved this problem when she bought a liquor store and had access to her alcohol every day of the week.

Fact: Family plays the biggest role in a person's likelihood of developing alcoholism. Children who are exposed to alcohol abuse from an early age are at a higher risk of falling into a pattern of abusive alcohol drinking.

Drinking while I was growing up caused a plethora of problems. To begin with, mother's drinking caused a love-hate relationship between us. Mother was controlling, vindictive, angry, lacked self-confidence and self-esteem and I was the victim of her behaviors. Consequently, I became fearful, isolated, depressed, anxious, and sought my parents' approval (which never happened.) I compensated by over-eating and felt the wrath of my mother for being "chubby."

Fact: Control is typically a reaction to the fear of losing control. People who struggle with the need to be in control often fear being at the mercy of others, and this fear may stem from traumatic events that left them feeling helpless and vulnerable. As a result, they may crave control in disproportionate and unhealthy ways. The experience of abuse or neglect, for example, can make people look for ways to regain control of their lives.

My childhood was tumultuous. I fought with my mother when she drank, and she drank every day. Her father, my maternal grandfather, was an alcoholic, a new immigrant to the United States and ruled the household with an iron hand. Her mother developed Parkinson's Disease in her mid-forties, was bed-ridden and also a tyrant. Mother, the eldest of five siblings, was responsible for the household chores and attending to her younger siblings. Her biggest desire was to leave home after high school graduation and attend nursing school to escape the throes of her parents.

World War II broke out during my mother's first semester of nursing school. She dropped out of school and joined the Women's Army Corps. She soon met my father; they were married within a few months, and he went off to the war. Mother was discharged from the military service when she told her commanding officer that she was pregnant (not true.) Needing a place to live, she moved to dad's hometown to live with his parents. Mother was Catholic; she drank, played cards, smoked, swore, and liked to fool around. Dad's parents were staunch Southern Baptist and they reacted like water and oil during the three years she was living with grandma and grandpa.

When dad returned home from the war, he and mother lived in Chicago where he attended radio school of some sort. I was born nine months later. Dad never finished radio school because of a lack of funds. They moved to dad's hometown in the Midwest. As far as I can remember, I never knew mother to be happy, unless she was drinking, which was most of the time.

Three years after they moved, my younger brother was born followed by a second brother and a sister within another three years. Mother didn't particularly want children and she told us nearly every day, "I never wanted any of you." This was a potent unloving and abandonment message for the four of us and we still feel the sting of her words as adults today.

I wasn't allowed to attend any high school social functions. I had no friends and was so very lonely. Mother and I fought constantly. She would grant me a day off from my household chores only to later deny me the time off. It made me feel as though I was going crazy. It was years later that I learned mother was having blackouts only to deny our conversation when she was sober. It was tough to be a kid in my house.

Fact: A drug-related blackout is a phenomenon caused by the intake of any substance or medication in which short-term and long-term memory is impaired, therefore causing a complete inability to recall the past.

I was brought up in the Catholic Church and attended parochial school. Grades one through eight were taught in a three-room red brick schoolhouse and we were taught by the nuns. By the time I was in fifth grade, I was asking a lot of "why" questions of the nuns about God and the most common answer was, "because I told you so." This was not good enough for me. I endured parochial school through the first semester of eighth grade when my parents took me out of school and enrolled me in the public school system.

As I grew older, I further doubted the Catholic Church and renounced their teachings. The first weekend I was away from home attending nursing school, I stopped attending church. For the next fifty years, I declared I was an agnostic. From time to time, I tried to read the bible, however, it made no sense to me. I had no prior exposure to its writings because the Catholic Church does not teach from the bible.

In my adult life, I was to meet three women who tried to convert me to Christianity. Try as I might, it wasn't working for me. Now I know I wasn't ready to be a Christian, although I longed for the peace these women had with their faith and that the Bible can't be understood without the Holy Spirit residing within us.

My childhood through my teen years was not atrociously horrible, but they were not pleasant only because I had learned to play mother's games. I never had a playful childhood. It wasn't until after mother's death at the age of sixty-five that I realized she parented her children as she was parented– the children did the household chores and she ruled with a strict ethic.

My father was also very strict and never went against mother's child-rearing decisions. Dad deprived me of any high school activities stating, "There will be boys there and I don't want you to get into trouble." It's my opinion that this was the beginning of my isolation. Although dad wouldn't let me participate in social events or date, he did allow me to work at the local theatre each Friday and Saturday night and Sunday afternoons. Now, that was a place where a kid could get into trouble.

Mother didn't tell what a young girl needed to know about monthly menstruation. I had no idea how a girl got pregnant until I was away at school, and I took an anatomy and physiology class. This parental neglect would later impact my first dating experience.

Not having school friends hurt and tore at my self-esteem. I can remember being eight or nine years old and sitting on the back porch of our house crying. Mother heard me and came out to sit with me.

"What's the matter," she asked.

Looking up at her with my tear-stained face and wet eyes, I asked her, "Why doesn't anyone like me?"

If I expected any comforting, it wasn't going to happen. Mother stood up and told me "I don't know. That's just the way it is."

Rejection and unloving and uncaring parents only added to my growing list of defects I was to identify later in my sobriety.

I was twelve and my oldest brother was nine years old when our parents took the two youngest siblings with them on a road trip in December to Pennsylvania, mother's home state. We were left alone for two weeks. It still amazes me how they thought it was okay to leave us unattended for this length of time. This was back in the 1950's and there weren't any cell phones. We set out a routine of eating breakfast, making our lunches, walking to school, doing homework, and eating dinner. I don't remember cooking, but I must have because we did eat. One snowy evening, I left my brother alone to go caroling with a group from school. It didn't occur to me to wear protective shoes on my feet because I suffered a mild case of frostbite on both feet. I was lucky that this was the worst thing that happened. The point is that children of this age don't have the maturity to make day to day decisions.

When I was fourteen years old, my family took a summer vacation in Red Rock, New Mexico, looking for a better climate for my brother's asthma. Dad went home after two weeks to return to work and mother stayed on for the summer with us. Her best friend lived nearby and was also an alcoholic making a great environment for us kids. On the drive home at the end of the summer, we stayed in a motel somewhere along the way. Mother needed a drinking companion, so she dressed me up and took me with her to the nearest bar. I was a little older and now she was introducing me as her sister, rather than her daughter. I was a bit confused with why I needed to be her sister.

The tension between me and my mother grew each day, and we could spend days without speaking to each other. I was falling into her growing up pattern of wanting and needing, to leave home as soon as possible after high school. I did, however, know that I needed to get an education to function on my own.

For as long as I could remember, I wanted to be a medical doctor. I studied hard and my grades were good. In my junior year of high school, I made an appointment with our school counselor. He reviewed my transcripts and felt I had a chance to get into one of the state university medical schools. All I had to do was to convince my parents.

The next day, I found my parents in the kitchen having their evening cocktail. Mother was stirring a pot of food for dinner. I very quietly and politely approached them.

"I was talking to Mr. Jones our school counselor about what I want to do when I graduate."

"That's nice," mother said without looking up from her cooking. Of course, dad showed no interest.

"I want to be a medical doctor and the counselor thinks I have a good chance of getting into medical school."

That caught both of my parents' attention and mother quit stirring her pot. Dad was the first to speak up, "Under no circumstances are you going to college. Only the boys will go to college."

"But, Dad, I have a nearly 4.0 grade point average and I've taken all the science classes that have been offered at school."

"You are not going to college and that is the end of the subject." I knew it was no use trying to talk with dad.

Mother tried to help the situation. "You can go to secretarial school and live at home."

"I'm not going to secretarial school. I want to be a doctor." I huffed and walked out of the room.

A few nights later, mother found me in my bedroom studying. "May I come in?"

"Of course," was my cold reply.

"I've been thinking about what you said the other night. That you want to go to medical school. You know that your father will stand by his decision that you aren't going to college?"

"I know, but there isn't anything else I want to do," I said looking up at her.

"Well, you could go to nursing school."

"I don't want to be a nurse. I want to be a doctor."

"Think about it," mother said as she left the room.

I decided that nursing school was my best, if only, option. I applied to a three-year hospital nursing school in Kansas City for the fall term. That summer, I received my acceptance letter.

Despite the differences I had with my mother, I must assume she went to bat with my father about going to school in Kansas City. They also agreed to pay my school expenses of $1,500 for thirty-six months. This amount of money paid for my tuition, room and board, uniforms, and books. I was ecstatic and started planning my move to leave home.

One evening at the dinner table, mother made an announcement. "Children, your father and I have made a decision." Such formality was uncommon in our household, and they got the attention of me, my sister and two brothers.

"We have decided to sell our house and move." There was dead silence while we absorbed what had just been said. Mother was proposing we move to a school rival town ten miles away.

"Do we get our own bedroom?" My younger brother asked who had been sharing his sleeping space with our other brother.

"No," Mother replied. "In fact, we'll be moving into a three bed-room house and the girls will share a bedroom as well as you boys."

"Mother, Dad, what about my school activities and my job?" I was nearly frantic because I was the editor of the high school yearbook and was on the debate team.

Dad looked at me and said, "You'll just have to adapt to the new high school."

"I'm not going to move, and you can't make me." I was sixteen years old and a senior in high school.

"Where are you going to live?" Mother asked.

"Why can't I live with grandma?"

Dad looked at mother and said, "You know that just might work." My grandfather had died six months earlier and grandma was living alone. "Sandy, do you want to talk to your grandmother?"

Without trying to show too much excitement, I told my parents I would talk with grandma after school the next day. Although my grandparents lived less than a block from us, we rarely saw them because of some unknown differences between them and my mother. When I knocked on her door the following afternoon grandma was surprised.

"Sandy, how wonderful to see you. Please come in, dear."

"Grandma, did you know mom and dad are going to sell our house and we'll be moving away?"

"Please sit down and tell me what's going on."

I relayed the announcement from the night before and that my entire senior year would be turned upside down.

"I was wondering if I could live with you until I graduate. I've already talk with mom and dad, and they told me I should talk with you."

Grandma gave me a wonderful smile and hug. "Sandy, I'm a lonely old lady and would love to have you live with me. You could have the first bedroom upstairs."

Elated, I ran up the stairs to see the bedroom. It had not been used in years and the closet was stacked with old magazines, papers, and boxes. The room and closet would need to be cleaned, but that was no problem.

I ran down the stairs, "Grandma that would be perfect. Can I move in this weekend?"

"If it's okay with your parents, I don't see any reason why you can't."

We talked about her expectations of a curfew and letting her know where I was and when I would be home. Since my parents had forbidden me to date, there weren't any concerns about boy issues.

The following weekend, I moved my clothes, books and stuffed dog, Harry, to my grandmother's house. Two weeks later, it was time for the family to move and mother and I were having another heated argument in the driveway as the last of their belongings were being loaded. She handed me twenty dollars and I refused it.

"I don't want your money. I have a job ushering at the theatre and I can support myself." I turned around and walked the block to my grandmother's house. In all honesty, I was hurt and felt rejected that they could leave me without a second thought. They didn't want me and in retaliation, I didn't want them.

I got to know my grandmother during the time I lived with her. She used to sit by her pot belly stove and make quilts by hand, sewing hundreds of squares together. When I took the time to sit and talk with her, she would tell me stories about how she and grandpa homesteaded in Oklahoma in 1907. Grandma had thirteen live births and lost four children either in childbirth or illness. How I wish I had taken the time to sit with her more often and write down her stories.

One day, I was looking through the stacks of papers in the closet of my bedroom and came across a piece of stationery embossed with the State Senate seal with my grandfather's name below the seal. I went downstairs and asked my grandmother about what I had found.

"Grandma, I found these papers and stationery in the back of my closet," I said as I handed her my findings. "Was grandpa really a state senator?"

Grandma took the papers from my hand and with a smile and tear in her eye said, "Yes, Sandy, he was in office for three terms. I had forgotten about these papers." Looking at me she said, "Thank you, Sandy."

"You're welcome. Will you tell me some stories about grandpa?" I was hungry to know more about my grandparents, especially when my parents didn't share any information with us, like my grandfather being a state senator.

"Perhaps another day." I could tell grandma was thinking of my grandfather.

I was very happy living with my grandmother and assumed I would live with her until I graduated. It wasn't long after I moved in with her that she began to have trouble swallowing. Being elderly and stubborn, she wouldn't go see a doctor.

"Dad, I am concerned about grandma," I began when I called him.

I told him about how her swallowing was getting worse and asked him to take her to a doctor. Dad took grandma to a specialist, and she was quickly diagnosed with cancer. She never returned home and died in a nursing home two months later. Once again, I had been abandoned. I didn't get to say goodbye to grandma.

There was no alternative other than to move in with my parents and give up my job at the theatre and high school activities. This was the second time my parents had moved me to another school.

The first time was when I was in eighth grade, and they transferred me from the parochial school with twelve students in my class to the public school system mid-semester where I knew none of the ninety classmates.

I was devastated this was happening again and became even more determined to leave home and go away to school after high school graduation.

Several weeks after receiving my acceptance letter for nursing school, mother and dad went their separate ways unannounced to anyone that they were leaving. My bubble about going away to school suddenly burst. I don't think my parents thought about what they were doing when they left home at the same time and abandoned their children. I was anxious, scared, and angry and I drank. I was the eldest and the only one of the kids who really had any idea of what had happened when my parents were absent from home. We were left with an old broken-down car which we used to get to school. I had fifty dollars in my savings account and didn't know how long that would last to buy groceries and gas. I also dreamt that I would have to quit school and be mother and father to my siblings, which was the last thing I wanted to do.

There was one thing I learned to do while they were away and that was how to drink down their liquor supply. I don't remember how many days they were gone. I do remember ironing on a Sunday afternoon when mother walked in the door. I was so angry all I could say was, "Where have you been?" Mother didn't answer me and walked directly into the bathroom. Not long thereafter, she came out and told me she had taken an overdose. Now, what did a seventeen-year-old know about overdoses? In a rage, I walked her around the house and poured coffee down her. She sat down on the sofa and fell asleep. She was breathing so I figured she hadn't been too affected by her alleged overdose.

Later that evening, dad came home. He had been in Texas with his brother. He took mother into their bedroom, and they were in there for some time. They never shared why they went their separate ways or why they didn't contact me to tell us they were okay. Nor did they apologize for the hell they put me through. In fact, the incident was never discussed.

In the spring of 1964, I graduated from high school and that summer I worked as a waitress in a local pancake restaurant. I'm not sure if I needed the extra dollars or if it was to convince myself I needed to get an education rather than wait tables for a living. I only had two months left before I would be leaving.

My Prayer

Heavenly Father, the past is the past and I've gone over it too many times. I was abandoned by my parents, especially my mother, while I was growing up. I know today that I am frightful of relationships because of a fear that I will be abandoned. Help me to learn to love and feel part of a relationship. In your Holy name, I pray.

CHAPTER TWO

Nursing School

Who has anguish? Who has sorrow? Who is always fighting? Who is always complaining? Who has unnecessary bruises? Who has bloodshot eyes? It is the one who spends long hours in the taverns, trying out new drinks. Proverbs: 23, 29-30

I was sitting in the back seat of our car with my parents in the front. We were driving to Kansas City, where I would attend nursing school. I still wasn't totally convinced that I wanted to become a nurse. But at least I would be in a related medical field and would be leaving home. I was seventeen years old.

I wasn't going to go away to school without Harry, my stuffed dog. I shut my eyes, hugged Harry, and remembered the scene at home just before we left. I was looking over my room to see if I had everything I needed when I saw dad and my oldest brother moving my bed out.

"What are you going to do with my bed?"

Dad didn't hesitate with his answer, "Since you won't be returning home, we sold your bedroom furniture."

This was incredulous to me. How could they sell my bedroom furniture, the desk I had spent hours at studying and the bed I had slept in for the past seventeen years? It was obvious to me that I wasn't welcome at home any longer. More abandonment.

This was the first time I had been away from home without my family. I found it exciting, scary, and unknown. I was to live in a dormitory with thirty other female freshman students for the next thirty-six months. Arriving at the dormitory, I quickly dismissed my parents after I was shown to my room. They wasted no time leaving. There were no hugs, tears, or goodbyes.

The house mother showed me to my room. I had arrived mid-morning so there wasn't much activity yet with other students showing up. There was a total of thirty freshman girls, and we were assigned two to a room. The house mother decided who was to room with whom. There really wasn't much to do to get settled in. We each had a twin bed, dresser, and desk. The community bathroom was down the hall. As afternoon approached, the hallways became loud with the voices of teenage girls introducing themselves and finding their assigned rooms. By the end of the afternoon, everyone was accounted for, except my roommate who wouldn't be arriving until the next day. And girls being girls, roommates tended to cling together. As I watched the commotion, I wondered if any of my classmates drank and how we would get booze into the dorm. I shouldn't have been too worried because it became apparent quickly who were the party girls.

Our schedule was grueling. We attended classes at the local community college in the mornings, had nursing classes at the hospital in the afternoon and worked on the wards after our first six months. My parents made the trip to Kansas City three times during my three years of schooling, and they brought me a case of liquor each time– no candy or cookies for this girl. Of course, this was so against the rules and would have gotten me expelled if I had been caught with liquor. Still, I found a way to hide the bottles and drank after the lights were out. I spent a good deal of time during my schooling without a roommate, so I was able to get away with this behavior.

I hadn't dated in high school and although I would love to meet a young man, my schedule prohibited it. One of my classmates approached me mid-semester and asked me if I'd like to go on a blind date with her and her fiancé. He and his friend, Ted, were dental students, and the school was having a big bon-fire with food and beer. I wasn't sure if I should go or not, but I would be with folks I knew. I had been so sheltered when I lived at home, that I wouldn't say 'no' to the invitation. Ted and I were quickly separated from our friends. We drank beer for a while and then he asked if I wanted to see his new car. I agreed and we walked to the parking lot. There stood a brand-new GTO– the hottest car of the year. "Would you like to get in?" Ted asked. "Sure" I replied as I climbed into the front seat. Ted wanted to make out and I didn't. When I refused, he out muscled me and before I knew what happened, he raped me. "See, that wasn't so bad, was it?" he said to me as I tried to arrange my clothes and torn shirt. I unlocked the car and ran to find my classmate. I don't know if they knew what happened with my torn shirt and bloody shorts. But they did take me back to the dorm quickly.

Not knowing anything about sex, pregnancy, or symptoms of pregnancy other than a missed period, I had convinced myself that I was pregnant because my period was late. I knew one of the other girls was familiar with a doctor that did abortions in his back room (this was in the days before abortions were legal.) She and her boyfriend took me to see the doctor and all the way there I was imagining a dirty back room and old instruments. The doctor was an older gentleman and by his demeaner I felt he had seen more than one teenager who thought she was pregnant. The doctor was very sympathetic and when he told me I was not pregnant, I hugged him.

Of the thirty students, twenty-seven lived in the Kansas City metropolitan area and they all went home on the weekends. Of the three that stayed in the dorm on weekends, two were from Iowa and then there was me and I was the only Catholic. The first weekend, I walked to church feeling guilty that I didn't want to attend Mass. I had pretty much denounced my faith while in high school and decided this was a good opportunity to quit going to church. After the first missed service it was very easy not to go to church after that.

The first weekend I went home, my folks loaded everyone in the car for church. "Uh, I quit going to church," I muttered thinking I could get out of the family outing. "If you are too sick to go to church, then you are too sick to be out of the house," my father looked me square in the face. I turned around and headed for the house. We never discussed attending church again.

Once we got to know each other better, there were three other classmates and myself that found a neighborhood bar about a mile from the dorm. The bar was frequented by college students and although we had to walk the mile, we felt safe as a group. We only had one problem and that was getting in and out of the dorm. As freshmen students, we had a curfew of 9pm during the week and 10pm on the weekends. We were required to sign out our destination and then sign in again when we returned to the dorm. There was no way we could sign out to a bar, so we decided to risk it and sneak in and out of the dorm.

There was a fire escape at the end of the hall and all we had to do was crawl out the window, climb down two flights of stairs and drop down a flight to the ground from the staircase. Getting back into the dorm was a little trickier as there was no way we could climb back onto the fire escape. The dorm was old and was the original hospital so when the new hospital was built, the older section was renovated as student nurse rooms with a single attachment of the dorm to the first-floor emergency room. For two months, we managed to get back into the dorm by sneaking through the Emergency Room without being caught. As odds would have it, the house mother was waiting for us one evening as we were sneaking back into the dorm. We knew we were in trouble and hoped that with the four of us, the punishment might be lighter. At 7am the following morning, we stood in our freshly washed and starched student nurse uniforms in front of the Director of Nursing. There was no discussion, no questions, only our sentencing of fifty demerits and being grounded to the dorm for six weeks. That escapade ended our trips to the bar.

There really wasn't much to do with what little free time we had, and we all became proficient at playing cards. I learned how to play Hearts and I already knew how to play Poker. During a heated game, one of the students told us she knew how to make homemade wine. How cool would that be to have a wine distillery.

The following weekend, we collected our wine making materials— a five-gallon glass container, grape juice, sugar, and a large balloon. Monday, we poured the grape juice and sugar into the glass container and affixed a balloon on the jar opening with a rubber band.

We knew we had to wait for the wine to ferment before we could drink it. Where to hide the fermenting wine? I chose to hide the wine in my room. By Friday the balloon had expanded. When I got back to my room that afternoon, I was greeted with a horrible odor. Looking into the closet, I discovered that the balloon had burst, and it was the fermented grape juice I was smelling. After alerting the other involved students, we opened windows, turned on fans and poured what was left of our wine down the drain. So much for easy access to wine.

Although my parents paid my tuition, I still needed some spending money to buy personal items such as hairspray, shampoo, and toothpaste. They solved this issue by depositing twenty dollars a month into my checking account. This worked well until my second year of school when I received a phone call from my dad.

"Sandy, you're overdrawn at the bank so we're cutting off your monthly allowance."

"How can that be? You taught me how to balance my checkbook to the penny and it has always balanced."

Dad wasn't willing to talk about how I was overdrawn, and my monthly stipend was gone. I again thought I was going to have to quit school and wait on tables. *"No, you aren't going to do that,"* I thought. *"There has to be a way."*

In desperation, I talked with one of my instructors about my situation. She told me that as junior students, we could work nights in the hospital as a nurse aide for money. This was great– I wouldn't have to quit school. I was, however, unprepared for the schedule I was about to embark upon.

During the day I was in class learning medical diagnosis and nursing skills such as giving a bed bath, administering medications, or taking care of patients on the wards. The evenings were devoted to the volumes of homework we were given. When the other students were going to bed for some much-needed sleep, I was reporting at 11pm on one of the wards where I worked until 7am. To this day, I don't know how I kept up with this routine.

We had thirteen months until graduation and were finishing up our nursing experience on the medical surgical wards, operating room, emergency room and geriatrics. The remainder of our three-year program would focus on obstetrics/gynecology, pediatrics, psychiatric and intensive care. I was becoming concerned that I was two-thirds through my training and hadn't found an area of nursing that I was crazy about. My first three-month specialty rotation was in the Intensive Care Unit. It didn't take long for me to discover this was going to be my area of expertise upon graduation. I loved the fast pace, acute illnesses and surgeries and exhilarated skill and knowledge levels that were required.

My next rotation was three months of obstetrics. The OB department was busy 24/7 and at a time when little in the way of pain medication was offered to the laboring mothers. There was also a shortage of beds which meant women were delivering babies on a gurney in the hallways. It was quite chaotic and not something I would choose to do every day. From there it was natural to slide into my pediatric days. I was totally surprised to find out that I enjoyed pediatrics and I did very well with my studies and skill sets. Although Peds was something I totally enjoyed, I knew that Intensive Care would be my calling.

My psychiatric training was spent at the State Mental Hospital. We were taken out of our hospital familiar environmental elements and sent to a mental hospital for three months. None of us knew what to expect and it was more than we imagined. The hospital was built in 1879 with the theory that good light and ventilation would be healthy for the patients.

Over the years renovations took place and, just like the hospital in Kansas City, the older patient rooms were used for student nurses. The furniture was metal and there was no carpeting on the floor. There were student nurses from all over the state and we found the time to get to know each other. Of course, I was interested in the drinking establishments in town. The students ahead of us had done the homework of finding a pub not far from the hospital. Nine or ten of us would hire cabs and go to the pub once or twice a week and play cards, drink beer and munch on snacks. Also inhabiting the bar were law students from the nearby law school. It was great to meet guys not associated with medicine. By this time, we had learned how to keep our drinking to a level so that we got a buzz on but managed to remain relatively sober.

At the end of our psych rotation, we returned to our dormitory buzzing with excitement. We had three months left before graduation and were finishing up class pictures, finalizing job offers, practicing graduation ceremony exercises, settling apartment contracts and, for some, planning weddings.

CHAPTER THREE

Leaving Kansas

I graduated from nursing school in August 1967 at the age of twenty. How ecstatic and proud I felt as I walked down the aisle in my new white uniform, cap, shoes, and nylons with no runs in them. Dad was sitting next to the aisle and winked at me as I passed him. He was the reason I was a graduate nurse, soon to be a registered nurse after taking the Kansas state nursing boards. Two conversations we'd had went through my head as I waited to be called up to the stage to receive my diploma and school pin.

"Dad, I hate school and want to quit," I cried into the phone midway through my first year.

"Kitten, you only have a few months in. Give it a year and see how you feel then."

I stayed in school and gave it 110% of my efforts. The second year was even tougher with my school responsibilities and working nights as a nurses' aide.

"Dad, I still hate school."

"Honey, you can't quit now. You only have a year to go."

Mother came to my graduation, and I was surprised because she missed most of my high school debates and theatre performances. What didn't surprise me was she didn't acknowledge the single most difficult thing I'd done in my short life– becoming a nurse.

Six months after I graduated, I had saved enough money from my job working in the Intensive Care Unit as a registered nurse (yes, I had passed my state boards) to leave Kansas City and venture out on my own. I packed what few belongings I had in my new car and drove to my hometown to say goodbye to my parents. Dad had two questions. Do you have enough money and where are you going? To the second question, I answered, "I don't know."

The next morning, I got in my car, pulled out of the driveway, and waved goodbye to my parents. I was off on the most exciting adventure of my life and didn't know where I would end up.

I drove sixteen hours that first day and marveled at the openness of the country, the red dirt of Oklahoma and the high buttes and plateaus of New Mexico. At sunset, I saw the most beautiful sky I had ever seen with its pinks and blues up against the statuesque red rocks. It rained most of that first day, but I wasn't deterred. When it wasn't raining, I drove with the windows down, what my dad called 4/70 air conditioning, and watched the scenery as I drove by. There's a whole lot of nothing in the desert to see, however, I found a great deal of beauty in the cactus, rocks, and clouds.

That first night was spent in Albuquerque. It was about 8pm when I drove into the town and along the highway were several hotels, but they all had 'no vacancy' signs light up. At the end of town, I made a U-turn and headed back to the last motel I'd seen– a Holiday Inn. Although there was a sign indicating there were no rooms available, I bravely parked my car in the rain and walked up to the front desk. I remember the clerk because he was fat and sleazy looking. Upon asking for a room, he gave me a grin as he leaned over the counter and said, "We're full, but I keep a room open in the back for some customers." I immediately knew he was trouble, said, "no thanks" and headed back to my car where I spent a short night sleeping.

The following morning as I drove west, I honestly couldn't believe I was on the road again, alone, and free. What would await me at my destination was unknown, but I was ready for anything. At the I-17 interchange in Flagstaff, I noticed a sign indicating Phoenix was 150 miles south. *"Why not,"* I thought to myself. *"I have to be somewhere, find a place to live and work. Why not Phoenix?"*

As I descended the northern mountains of Arizona and came down in altitude, the scenery changed from pines to open land with saguaro cactus and brush. It was beautiful and I was mesmerized.

My drinking had not been unreasonable up to now. Mostly because I was working during the evenings, saving money to move and I didn't make a lot of money. However, that was about to change.

CHAPTER FOUR

Phoenix

Everything seemed to fall into place when I drove into Phoenix. I wasn't in town long when I saw a garden style apartment complex for singles. Bingo, I had hit pay dirt as long as I could afford it. The fellow in the manager's office was wonderful and friendly and told me they had a studio for $110 a month, or a one bedroom for $140 a month. In 1968 that $30 was a big difference, so I asked to see the studio. It so reminded me of the dorm room I had lived in for three years, but I decided to take it anyway.

The young folks at the pool came to meet me and helped me move in. Thirty minutes later, I was in the pool with a bottle of beer. I couldn't believe my luck in finding such a fun place to live and drink.

Three days later, I found a job working in the Intensive Care Unit on nights. There was no way I was going to turn the job down and would wait for a position to open up on days. I soon found out that I now couldn't sleep in the morning after working all night. I started having a couple of beers to make me sleepy, however, that didn't always work. Then I began to stop at a local bar for drinks when I got off my shift to counteract the loneliness I was feeling.

I worked with a nurse named Ella. The first night I reported to work at 11pm, I got report on the patients from the two evening nurses. There was no Ella, and I was left alone to take care of four critically ill patients. After report, the two nurses got ready to leave. "You can't leave me alone with these patients." I pleaded. "Sorry, but we've covered for Ella too long and now that you're here, we're going to leave." And leave they did. An hour later, Ella came staggering in, put her coat and purse on the counter, sat down in a chair, said "Hello" and promptly passed out. By shift change, she'd had enough sleep that she could face the oncoming day nurses with a smile. It went on like this for two weeks before I'd had enough and reported her to my supervisor. Ella got fired and the incident didn't register with me that I could be in Ella's place in a few years.

Not long after getting settled in my studio apartment, I started dating a fellow named Joe who lived below me on the first floor. Joe was an accountant, worked from home and he loved to drink. This was okay with me because he always paid for our entertainment. It didn't take me long to figure out the reason he worked from home was he got to drink all day. Many years later, I learned that he died of his alcoholism at the age of forty-three. He did introduce me to Scotch which became my drink of choice.

A girl from the apartment complex suggested we go to the Playboy Club one Friday night. I was up for most anything and agreed to go. What an awakening this country girl got when we walked into the Playboy. There were girls in bunny suits with little on top. Drinks were easy to get because the Bunnies carried them throughout the room. That first night, I met a young attorney. He was very handsome and asked me to go with him and a group of friends to Rocky Point, Mexico, for the weekend. How could I say no? The only problem was I was scheduled to work that weekend. I had a friend call in sick for me and I didn't worry about the consequences. What a weekend. We drank and drank some more for forty-eight hours straight. I parasailed behind a jeep that drove along the beach. We cooked on an open fire, and everyone was making out with everyone else. My mind is still fuzzy about what happened that weekend with all the booze that was floating around. When I returned to work on Monday night, I was summoned to the head nurse's office and called on the carpet for not personally calling in sick. I nearly lost my job for those two incredible days of fun.

A year later, I made a quick weekend trip to San Diego with a girl I'd met at the apartment. I had never seen the Pacific Ocean and fell in love with the entire beach scene. She knew a real beach bum named Paul who lived in a shack on the beach, and I was immediately in love– with Paul and the beach. Paul looked just like a California beach bum– tanned, muscles, blond hair, blue eyes, and a famous California beach smile. It didn't take long for him to invite us for dinner.

"Hey, why don't you two girls stay for dinner? I'll cook for you."

"How are you going to cook, I don't see a stove or pots and pans?" I asked smiling and looking around.

He gave me his gorgeous California smile and said, "I'll build a fire on the beach, and we'll grill the fish I caught today."

I was already on a high with the new things I was experiencing. As the sun went down, Paul started a fire, cleaned some corn on the cob and buttered a yummy looking loaf of sour dough bread. Paul handed me a small drink glass. "What is this?" I asked.

"Sake."

"What is Sake?"

"It's a Japanese wine made of fermented rice. It'll sneak up on you, so drink it slowly."

"Do you have any ice?" I asked.

"Nope, you drink sake at room temperature."

I wasn't too crazy about the Sake and was thankful when Paul opened a bottle of Chardonnay wine.

Soon after dinner, my friend was asleep. Paul and I walked down to the beach. I took off my shoes so I could feel the sand and water squish through my toes. It was all so romantic. Paul and I sat on the shore, and we opened a new bottle of wine. At some point, I fell asleep and didn't wake up until the following morning when the sun was up, and the waves were lapping at my feet. There was no doubt that I would be moving to San Diego just as soon as I could save enough money. Oh yes, I never saw Paul again and that was okay.

C H A P T E R   F I V E

San Diego

Six months later, I left Arizona and moved to San Diego. I was on a quest for adventure and fun. This was a great time in my life. I met guys, played in the ocean, body surfed and snorkeled the waves, bar hopped, partied, and drank. I lived in Pacific Beach, so I was in the middle of party town. Beer was the choice of drinks back in those days because we were young and short on cash. We didn't consider beer drinking (as most people didn't) so it wasn't a problem.

It was during this phase of my life that I experienced my first blackout. I attended a party after I got off my shift at midnight. I drank a lot of alcohol over a short period of time to catch up with the other party people. When I woke up the following morning I was confused as to how I got home, if my car was in one piece, and if I was alone in bed. To this day, I have no idea how I drove the thirty miles home without getting into an accident. And, yes, I was alone in my bed.

Marijuana was growing in popularity at this time. I refused all offers to smoke because I didn't want to get addicted. Little did I realize I was already addicted to alcohol?

A year after I moved to California, I quit my night job working in the Intensive Care Unit and went to Europe for six weeks with a nurse I didn't know well and who didn't drink. I had been bar hopping alone for a couple of years and knew I could visit the pubs in Europe without a partner. During our travels, I discovered European wines, such delicate liquids. I added another alcoholic substance to my growing list of mood enhancers.

We happened to arrive in Munich, Germany one evening in a downpour of rain during the famous Oktoberfest. We lucked out finding a room across from the fair. After dropping off our bags, we ventured across the street. It was crazy with people drinking beer from huge steins and the barmaids carrying three and four steins in each hand. The Ferris Wheel was busy, chickens were roasting on spits, and everyone was singing. We spoke no German but did manage to order a stein of beer. As we were walking around, we noticed three nice looking men about our age. They approached us first and we learned, through some sort of sign language that they were off duty police officers. We spent the remainder of the evening with these charming men, drinking, singing, and dancing in the rain. We left the next day to return to the States– what a great send off.

After returning from Europe, I decided to move to San Francisco, the hub of dining and drinking. Little did I know that it truly was the loneliest city. I was once again working nights at a well-known university hospital. Although I had marvelous experience working with heart patients, I was lonely and spent a great deal of my time drinking when I wasn't working. It took me six months to save enough money to move back to San Diego.

I returned to San Diego on a wonderful, warm weekend in June. With another increase in salary, I rented an apartment not far from the beach. I was truly happy again and that Sunday morning while I was doing my laundry, I met a fellow who would become my first husband. He was a handsome man with an exciting career in the FBI. I wanted to meet this person who was doing his own laundry, so I tried to stage drying my clothes as close to his dryer as possible. If he hadn't folded his clothes twice, we might not have met. Here I was in jean shorts, a crop top, and my hair in two long ponytails when I walked into the laundry room. We had a little

"Hi, how are you," conversation before he asked if I'd like to come up to his apartment for a cup of coffee. I was delighted and without showing too much excitement accepted his invitation. After I took my laundry home, I put on some lipstick and knocked on his door.

Josh was his name, and he did offer me that cup of coffee. Surprisingly enough, he was drinking a beer at nine in the morning. I would much rather have had the beer but didn't want Josh to think I drank a lot. We spent the day together and by noon, we were both drinking. We made plans to go out to dinner that night and it became a late night which would have been okay except I was starting a new job the next day at six in the morning. I woke up at 5am and just barely made it on time to work.

Josh and I saw a lot of each other over the ensuing months. Each outing we had was accompanied by a lot of drinking. We also had some rocky times that I can now attribute to the fact we both drank too much and argued as often. If we had known better, we would have never gotten married, but we did. We had a wonderful wedding in San Diego and spent our Honeymoon in Hawaii. Unfortunately, marriage didn't slow down our drinking, or the arguments and we were divorced six years later.

During the time Josh and I were married, I left working as an Intensive Care Nurse and entered the field of Occupational Health Nursing. The advantage was that I was now working days with weekends off. I had time on my hands with my new job and decided it was time for another challenge. With one phone call, I enrolled in the local Nurse Practitioner Program at the university. It was another whirlwind two years of school, working and maintaining a social life. I graduated with a state certification as a nurse practitioner and later received my national certification.

During the time I was in school, I met an engineer named Beau. We became great friends and our friendship evolved to morning coffee before work and I soon confided in him about my failing marriage. We began to fall in love and when my divorce from Josh was final, we bought a house and moved in together. Beau drank very little, and he completely quit drinking soon after we started living together. This didn't stop me from drinking, but it did slow me down for the next couple of years.

Not long after Beau and I settled in our new home, having completed the nurse practitioner program, I once again returned to school, finished my undergraduate degree, and started on my graduate degree which was interrupted by a new job offer. I had been engaged in workers 'compensation administration in my job duties in occupational health. I had also been aggressive in learning my job and soon knew enough to be scouted by a large insurance company in San Francisco. Their job offer truly put me over the top. I had the title of Director and traveled throughout California, Arizona, and Alaska. This was in the 1980's when companies still paid for liquid libations at company functions and travel expenses. On my trips, we ate at only the finest eating establishments and drank the best liquor.

It was during a week-end retreat that I experienced my second blackout. We were meeting at a large resort situated along the shoreline in Newport Beach, California. The agenda was golfing the first afternoon. For those of us who didn't play golf, drinking was the second choice. I was happy to oblige the second choice. Around 4pm, folks were dwindling back to the hotel for a much-needed nap. That was fine with me because the sun and liquor had caught up with me and I needed a break to be clear-headed for the first meeting beginning at 7pm that evening. The meeting was short and there was an introduction to the agenda the following day. After dessert, I followed the group into another room set up for playing Poker. There was no doubt card playing was the plan for the remainder of the evening. I may not play golf, but I could play Poker. After three hours, my card playing got risky– yes, we were playing for money– and I decided it was time to go to my room for the rest of the evening. I remember fumbling for my hotel key and having trouble getting into the room. The rest of the night is a complete blur– the walk from the dining area, passing out on the bed, dropping my sweater in the hallway on the way back, sleeping completely clothed and waking up not knowing where I was. That was my second blackout and it scared me. I lost hours out of my life that night and I still have no recollection of what happened.

When I got home, I emptied every liquor bottle in the house. The blackout was a wakeup call for me. It was time I quit drinking before I got hurt or hurt someone else.

I was sober for the next seven years. Not drinking wasn't that difficult because my husband didn't drink, and we didn't socialize with folks who drank. In 2003, the Cedar Fire of San Diego caused us to evacuate our home for a week. We spent the first two days in an abandoned parking lot and the rest of the time with my husband's brother east of San Diego where the threat of fire was low. When we arrived at his home, the first thing Jerry asked me was, "Would you like a glass of wine?" I didn't even hesitate and said "Yes." Jerry and I drank two bottles of wine that afternoon. About 5pm, the guys went on an errand. I found an unopened bottle of Johnnie Walker Red Scotch, hid the bottle in my suitcase and finished it off before retiring for the evening. All it took was one glass of wine, an invitation, my guard down and I was right back to drinking as much as I used to.

Why was I so weak that I couldn't resist that glass of wine and/or felt I was strong enough to have just the one glass? I had no belief in God and my husband was no support in reminding me I had taken a vow with myself never to drink again. That's what alcoholics do. They break promises, especially with themselves and with those they love. That wine and Scotch were sweeter nectar than the promises I had made.

> *Fact: I'm convinced that every destructive behavior and addiction I battled off and on for years is rooted in my insecurities.*

Five years after the Cedar Fires, we moved to northern Arizona to retire. We had talked at length about retiring to the mountainous area and after an exhaustive search, we found land and built our dream home. This was really a bittersweet decision because my husband was diagnosed with cardiovascular disease and had three stints placed in his heart a year before we moved. In spite of his health, he still wanted to relocate. I was ecstatic because ever since I had left Arizona in my twenties, I knew I'd return some day.

CHAPTER SIX

Northern Arizona

Beau became a cardiac recluse and within three years of moving to northern Arizona had two more stints placed in his heart and ultimately a Coronary Artery Triple Bypass Graft. All communication stopped between us and he essentially pulled away from me. My past and my health career told me I should be able to do something to save him from his impending death, but I didn't know what that should be. Again, I had no faith in God and couldn't understand why my husband's death was so terrible.

The sicker Beau became, the more depressed I became, and I spent a great deal of my alone time drinking. One day I picked up a new prescription of Vicodin and had a multitude of anti-depressant medications at my disposal at home. I truly wanted to leave this world. There was nowhere else to go and no one to turn to. To this day, I remember looking at the pills and thinking, *"What the hell."* I swallowed all the Vicodin tablets and as many of the other pills as I could and washed them down with red wine.

I was aware of slumping over my computer as I became drowsier and drowsier until I went into a coma. The following morning my husband found me unresponsive, non-breathing, no discernible pulse and my body didn't register a temperature. He called 911 and I was admitted to the ICU where I remained in a coma for three days. The ER doctor told Beau I had arrived at the Emergency Room DOA (Dead on Arrival.)

Dying was the easiest thing I've ever done. It was peaceful and without pain. As I drifted into unconsciousness, I knew I had done the right thing and was not remorseful about my actions. At some point in my coma, I felt myself rising above my body and saw myself lying in the hospital bed. I didn't hear singing, I didn't see angels or any other heavenly figures; however, I know I had an out of body experience. Waking up was abrupt and frightening. I so wanted to return to the peaceful place I had found.

I was transferred to a psychiatric detoxification facility in Phoenix where I remained under observation for ten days. I had no idea what I was doing there and was never told it was a detoxification unit. I ate, slept, and had three meetings with a psychiatric person who was more interested in asking me if I knew why I was admitted than trying to get to the root of why I was there. When I got home, life returned to its usual uncommunicative state, and I returned to drinking. The only difference this time was that I was now hiding my wine and Scotch thinking my husband wouldn't know I was drinking. In all actuality, I don't think he cared because he was dealing with his own medical and emotional issues.

> *And you will say, "They hit me, but I didn't feel it. I didn't even know when they beat me up. When will I wake up so I can have another drink?" Proverbs 23:35*

Beau never recovered from his surgery and spent the last twenty-one days of his life in the Intensive Care Unit with me by his side. It was a sad and lonely death because he suffered total body failure and was intubated all but the last day before he passed. If I wasn't at the hospital, I was at a local bar looking for company and attention. My husband had shut me out. Obviously, he didn't need me.

My dad died six weeks after Beau died. I became an emotional wreck and drowned my sorrows in alcohol. I have always been somewhat of a thrill seeker and now drove my sports car recklessly over tortuous mountain roads while drinking. I took up shooting and, under the influence of alcohol, did practice shooting on the off roads in the country. I bought a new Corvette and engaged in track racing. Hoping to meet men, I joined a couple of on-line dating sites which turned disastrous. I was amazed at how many men in their sixties and seventies didn't drink. This didn't work for me.

I was very lonely and missed my husband terribly. At the suggestion of a lady friend, I had a blind date with someone she knew. Knowing I was a bit hesitant she said, "You'll be okay. He's fun, has money and loves to drink and dance."

My friend was right, he was fun, had money and loved drinking and dancing. I was so blinded by loneliness that I didn't see the signs of alcoholism, emotional abuse, and eventually physical abuse. We both drank too much, and his comment was, "If I'm an alcoholic, so what? I'm nearly eighty years old and I'm not going to quit now."

I had also made the big mistake of moving into the house next door to him. Not a good idea. This only made getting out of the living arrangement harder and more complicated. When I broke up with him, I was desperate and moved at the age of seventy to a small town in central Arizona in hopes of starting over again. *My life would change drastically a year later.*

I didn't meet many people after moving and became more and more isolated. The more isolated I became, the more depressed I became. The more depressed I became, the more suicidal thoughts I had.

> *Fact: An alcoholic may seek a life of isolation for a number of reasons including denial, rejection, anger, and fear. They may be suffering from an undiagnosed co-occurring mental illness such as depression, social anxiety, or paranoid personality disorder.*

Even when I was in a group of people, I felt lonely. In my lonely state, I felt insecure and would take my drink and retreat to the outside of the room where I didn't have to interact with anyone.

> *Fact: Alcoholism and social isolation are intrinsically linked. This is due to the fact that the alcoholic will remove all obstacles to his or her drinking behaviors or patterns, including socializing with friends and family. As the alcoholism progresses, the alcoholism and social isolation become more pronounced, often resulting in the alcoholic planning their entire day around being home, often alone, with free rein to drink with no accountability to others.*

There was something pulling at me to learn about God and Christianity. I didn't know what it was, but I desperately needed peace. I was talking to a Christian woman who lived in my neighborhood, and she suggested I talk with the pastor of her church. That was okay with me as long as they would come to my house, and I didn't have to meet in a church. The following week, both the senior and associate pastors came calling for a visit. I expressed my need for peace and shared my past history of Catholicism and then no faith. I also told them I had tried to read the bible to no avail. We set forth a plan that the associate pastor and his wife would return and introduce me to the Bible. Of course, I was invited to services at the church. I had three meetings with the associate pastor and his wife and surprised myself at how much I knew about the Bible's writings. There were no plans at the conclusions of these meetings, however, I managed to set other things in motion.

I was invited to a social evening event given by the Bible Study group of the church my friend attended. My friend picked me up and when we arrived, I soon learned there was no liquor, and I desperately wanted/needed a drink. I told my friend I wasn't feeling well, and could she take me home, which she cordially did. I had gotten myself so isolated internally at the party that I was worked up into a frenzy by the time I got home. Naturally, my first reaction was to find some liquor in the house as soon as my friend left.

There is no way I can describe the feelings and thoughts I undergo when I drink, and my brain chemistry gets completely out of whack. My head says "*die*" and my heart says "*why?*" I can't make sense of any reasonable thoughts and all I want to do is drink, take some pills and die.

An Alcoholic Brain

I've been off and out of sorts— again,
My brain chemistry feels off balanced.
Nerve cells don't synapse correctly,
Neurons don't transmit information succinctly.

Mitochondria are slow to produce energy.
DNA is dog-tired,
ATPs are in short supply,
Information to the brain is out of whack.

Where is my dopamine?
Serotonin forgot to come to work,
I felt excited when I had glutamate,
Norepinephrine kept me stress-free.

Feelings of wanting to leave this world,
Unworthiness, low self-esteem, abandonment,
Feeling unloved, not being enough,
Have crept back into my life.

I can't make sense out of living,
I've never known happiness or joy.
Peace, kindness, and grace,
Are eluding me.

I want to feel balanced,
I want to love myself,
I want to want to live,
I want to feel alive.

Some might say that I should have fought off the temptation to drink and take pills. This may sound okay to the non-addictive brain, but that's not the way my brain works when I drink. I felt that I had no choice, nor would anyone miss me when I was gone.

I took the pills and drank the Scotch. I didn't feel drowsy at first but thought I should lie down just in case I had taken enough for life to end.

I'm not sure how long I was out. When I woke up my first thought was, *'I'm not dead.'* It was then that I heard a voice.

"You will not die, for I have plans for you to serve me."

I instantly knew this was the voice of God. How I had yearned to know God and come to peace with myself and those around me. And there He was, talking directly to me. The joy, peace and love I felt at that instant was incredibly overwhelming. I knew then that Jesus Christ had forgiven me my sins and rescued me from Satan. I held my hands to my chest over my heart and felt the wonder of the Holy Spirit enter my body. My friends, there are so few words to describe this happening. Not everyone is as fortunate as I was to feel God and the Holy Spirit in a Spiritual Awakening such as I did.

I suddenly had the uncontrollable urge to vomit and expel liquid feces at the same time. I spent many minutes over the toilet before I could call my friend seeking help. When I reached her by phone, all I could say was, "I'm in trouble." She was there in minutes, called 911, and I was taken to the Emergency Room. While I was being seen in the Emergency Room, my friend was busy behind the scenes. She called her pastor and explained the situation. They then got in contact with a drug and alcohol mental health therapist from the church. Once I was discharged from the Emergency Room and seen by a nurse practitioner in the clinic, I was whisked off to the therapist. He must have been given my history by my friend because the first thing he said to me was, "You're an alcoholic."

This was the first time I had been called an alcoholic and the seriousness of it hit me squarely in the gut. He arranged for me to be admitted to a detoxification center for five days and then admitted to a drug and alcohol in patient treatment program for four weeks. The total fee for detoxification and treatment was $66,000 and needed to be cash up front. I depleted my savings and was granted admission to the treatment centers. Today, I remain sober and a recovering alcoholic.

I was hungry for God and a feeding of my soul. That, however, wouldn't happen until I had completed my treatment program and returned home to my environment where I would have the time and a dedicated place to begin to learn about God.

After a lifetime of not believing, I'm now a Christian. My heart has been changed by the presence of God and I no longer desire my old ways of living. I thank God every day for my sobriety and my new life. I strive to be in fellowship with God, to be filled with His love and to bring glory to Him. I feel the peace I witnessed in those Christian women who had the faith in me that I could become a Christian and place my life in the hands of God.

My Prayer

Heavenly Father, I have lived a life of isolation, depression, and despair. Growing up, I questioned if that was as good as it gets. I know now that the best it can get is your love and acceptance of who I am, not who I want to be or who I thought I was. My Beloved Lord, please be with me as I live through the stages of recovery knowing each day will be different and not always easy. I beseech you to stay with me and lead me on the road to sobriety fighting the ever-present Satan along the way.

> *Jeramiah 29:11 "For I know the plans I have for you, declares the Lord. "Plans to prosper you and not to harm you, plans to give you hope and a future."*

CHAPTER SEVEN

Recovery

Addiction and Recovery

Addiction changes who you are and how you think,
You find the world becomes a puzzle of confusion in a wink.
One day you find a new friend named Recovery,
You become wiser and stronger in your discovery.

With Recovery, you learn to laugh and play,
The world is no longer shades of gray.
You learn more about your addiction,
Shame and guilt become past afflictions.

You own your story by telling it to others,
It's one of your new life wonders.
You found different friends and hobbies.
They are sober, fun, and not so naughty.

You needed to cry and found the tears,
Tears of unwantedness over the years.
You wanted to live to face another day,
You soon found the courage to stay.

You deserve the person you have become,
Because you fought to become her.

I was discharged from the treatment center after four weeks of inpatient therapy. I won't say that therapy was an easy road however each day was a better day without alcohol. We spent a lot of time in group therapy learning about our addictions and how we would handle those defects when we returned to our outside world without protective walls.

In April 2011 the American Society of Addiction Medicine (ASAM) released its new Definition of Addiction, which, for the first time, extends addiction to include behaviors other than problematic substance abuse. The Society concluded that addiction is about the underlying neurology of the brain not about outward behavior.

In the past, diagnosis of addiction has focused on outward manifestations of a person's behaviors, which can be observed and confirmed by standardized questionnaires. The new definition of addiction instead focuses on what's going on inside you, in your brain.

The experts at ASAM hope their new definition leads to a better understanding of the disease process, which they say is biological, psychological, social, and spiritual in its manifestation.

Traditionally, people with addictions have sought and received treatment for a particular substance or behavior. This has sometimes resulted in the person substituting one addiction for another—what ASAM calls the "pathological pursuit of rewards"—because the underlying cause was not treated. ASAM suggests that comprehensive addiction treatment should focus on all active and potential substances and behaviors that could be addictive. ASAM was careful to point out that the fact that addiction is a primary, chronic brain disease does not absolve addicts from taking responsibility for their behaviors.

I couldn't remember when I felt happy, at peace or free. In recovery, I was being given the tools to be that person. All I needed to do was to remain sober and live each day at a time. I deserve recovery, I deserve to be happy, I deserve to be at peace, I deserve to be free.

CHAPTER EIGHT

More Facts About Alcoholism

Abdonment

Abandonment has had a huge impact on me in both my childhood and adult life. My parents would leave their four children home alone for hours and days for their own pleasure. We were expected to function alone without adult supervision. When my parents thought I was old enough at the age of twelve, they began to leave us for longer periods of time.

With abandonment comes a feeling of being unloved. There was never a show of affection in our home. My parents never hugged or kissed in front of us. As for us kids, I can only remember one hug from dad and when he realized what he was doing, he withdrew embarrassed.

Facts: Not loving children makes them feel insecure, ugly, incapable of learning and forming relationships in their childhood that extends into adulthood.

It's always been difficult for me to form relationships wondering and mistrusting why someone would like to be my friend. When I was older,

I was unsure of dating and what the rules of dating were. When I realized that an ounce or two of alcohol would help me feel more comfortable around singles and small crowds of people, I always made sure I had that drink before I left the house and that there would be drinking at the function. I'd watch to see how much my date drank and made sure I never had more to drink that he had.

Facts: Addicts are likely to experience trauma and abuse as a child. Abuse and neglect (abandonment) deepens mistrust of others and further distorts reality. Children who are neglected conclude they are not valuable and are unloved. In addition, they live with a high level of anxiety because no one teaches them common life skills or provides for their basic needs. Children find ways to deaden the anxiety they feel.

I found alcohol deadened how deprived I felt. How could I be a mother to my siblings? How could I have enough money to support my little family? Would I have to quit school, find a job, and never have a bright future? I no longer trusted my parents to take care of us and was always on the alert for inadequacies in their promises.

Genetics

There has been much discussion whether alcoholism is a genetic disease or an environmentally influenced disease– or both. Research shows that multiple genes play a role in a person's risk for developing Alcohol Use Disorder (AUD.) Fifty percent of alcoholism is associated with genetics. Environmental factors, as well as gene and environmental interactions account for the remainder of the risk. (National Institute of Alcohol Abuse and Alcoholism)

Alcoholism seems to run in families. According to the American Academy of Child& Adolescent Psychiatry, children of alcoholics are four times more likely than others to become alcoholics. Family and adoption studies have shown that alcoholism definitely has a genetic component.

Fact: Alcoholism is a disease that does not discriminate and can impact anyone. Alcohol dependence can form quickly and aggressively, or it may surface over a longer period of time.

Considering the association I formed with alcohol, my alcoholic genes were expressed early in my life.

My Prayer

Lord, Jesus Christ, there are things in this life that we can control. And those we can't. Surely, our inherited traits and characteristics are those that are uncontrollable, and it is my responsibility to accept and learn to use them in a productive way.

Isolation and Depression

A lot of people who suffer from alcoholism also suffer from isolation. The two tend to go hand in hand. I've isolated most of my life and the more and longer I drank, the more I felt the need to isolate myself from my environment and people. I remember in my earlier drinking days, I would prefer to stay home rather than mingle because I never felt good enough, smart enough or worthy enough to socialize with others. With a few drinks, these "enough" feelings would subside until I had "enough" to drink and then it really didn't matter.

My personal isolation grew to the extent that I couldn't face leaving the house to interact with others. I declined social invitations making up excuses to avoid being with others or having people in my house. One of my biggest fears was answering the door and my liquor bottles, or glasses would be visible to the person on the other side of the door.

Fact: It is estimated that up to as many as 20 percent of people who receive treatment for alcoholism also have a social anxiety disorder. This disorder is characterized by the excessive fear of social situations and social settings. The disorder ranges from mild anxiety to severe anxiety that can cause a person to shun the outside world and be housebound.

Alcohol's depressant nature dampens the pleasure center of your brain which not only leads to depression but enables self-isolation, self-pity, catastrophic thinking, and self-destructive patterns in the brain. Someone once said, "In an alcoholic state, alcohol is seen as the primary relationship in that person's life." That is just how I felt when I was drinking.

My Prayer

Holy Father, You know how easily I become isolated and how self-destructive this can be for me. As I go through the stages of recovery, I am asking You to guide me in meeting new people and trying new activities.

Physiology

When you take a drink of alcohol, it goes directly to the stomach and then to the small intestine where most of the alcohol gets absorbed into the blood stream. Alcohol then travels in the blood stream to the liver where it gets metabolized. Another portion of the alcohol goes to the brain where it impacts the part that controls judgement, memory, speech, movement, and communication. That's why people who drink too much have poor judgement, memory, slurred speech and become "fallen down drunk."

We've all either seen people who've had too much to drink or have been there too often ourselves. Once a person drinks to excess over a period of time, the frontal lobe of the brain is affected which is the part of the brain that allows you to think normally.

Alcohol can also cause pancreatitis, cancer, and fetal alcohol disorders if you drink while you are pregnant.

> *Fact: Women's bodies absorb and make use of chemicals differently than men. Women have more body fatty tissue proportionately than men. Alcohol gets absorbed more slowly by fat which keeps the alcohol in a woman's bloodstream longer making it more toxic for women.*

As the years passed, my tolerance to alcohol increased so that I rarely got high or appeared to be drunk.

> *Fact: Tolerance is a condition of getting so used to a drug that the body needs more or it to have the same pleasurable effects.*

> *My Prayer*

My beloved Lord, please be with me as I live through the stages of recovery knowing each day will be different and not always easy. I have abused prescription drugs in the past and am adding this addiction to alcohol abuse in my recovery.

CHAPTER NINE

The Twelve Steps A Blueprint to Recovery

You have to fight through some bad days to earn the best days of your life.

The Twelve Steps of Alcoholics Anonymous were first developed in 1939 by the founders of AA, Bill W. and Dr. Bill as they are affectionately referred to. These steps were written by men, for men's needs in recovery while women had few resources and little political, social, or economic power. It's only been in the past twenty years that attention has been paid to the issues of the alcoholic woman and that recovery means something different to her. Although there has been an effort to rewrite the Twelve Steps by women, for women, the Steps and the structure of the program does offer women the opportunity to explore recovery from addiction as empowered women.

In the "Big Book"—the central text of AA that outlines the program—the twelve steps are defined as a "set of principles, spiritual in nature, when practiced as a way of life, can expel the obsession to drink and enable the sufferer to become happily and usefully whole.

"We couldn't, He could, so we let Him"

Step One

Step One- "We admitted we were powerless over alcohol– that our lives had become unmanageable."

When I first read Step One, I had no idea what it meant. How could I be powerless over alcohol? After all, I felt powerful when I drank. I could afford the tremendous financial drain of drinking. I had drinking friends who drank as much as I did. No one was telling me to quit drinking. There was no way I could accept that I was powerless over alcohol. I was a very strong and determined woman who accomplished many goals in life. I didn't need, or want, to feel powerless.

In my rehabilitation program, we amazingly didn't spend much time on the Twelve Steps, so when I got out and returned home to resume my life without my longtime friend, Alcohol, I started reading about alcoholism. I read and read and read some more. As I began to understand my disease, the concept of powerlessness became clearer. For me, it was the inability to not drink, or to even cut back on my drinking. I enjoyed alcohol, the taste and feeling it gave me. Who had power? Alcohol or me? As we all know, including myself, power cannot be had over alcohol. It changes our thinking, our behavior, our self-esteem, our relationships and how we live our life. As addicts, we simply cannot live without alcohol in our lives. We are powerless over whether we drink or don't drink.

Now that I understand powerlessness as it relates to alcoholism, it doesn't have the negative stigma it originally implanted in my brain. Powerlessness is a part of being an alcoholic, much as dancing is part of being a dancer. You can't separate the two.

I thought I was managing my life very well while I was drinking. Through the recovery process, I examined my drinking years and came to the abrupt conclusion that I couldn't manage my life if I was drinking. And if I wanted to, I didn't manage it very well. I sought out bars for entertainment. I dated men who drank and drank a lot. If there wasn't alcohol available,

I would stay home so that I could drink. These activities didn't bring me any joy or happiness. My life was in a state of unmanageability.

I didn't start learning how the Twelve Steps applied to me until I attended AA meetings after I left my rehabilitation program. As I listened to the testimonies of other AA members, I began to understand the meaning of Step One.

The principle behind Step One is honesty and I couldn't proceed to Step Two until I honestly admitted that I was powerless over alcohol and that my life was unmanageable. That being accomplished, I moved on to Step Two.

Step Two

Step Two- Came to believe that a Power greater than ourselves could restore us to sanity.

> *And I know that nothing good lives in me, that is, in my sinful nature. I want to do what is right, but I can't." Romans 7:18*

I had never believed in a Power greater than myself. I spent years asking God to reveal Himself to me. I wanted the peace and serenity I had seen in women who had faith. Why couldn't I believe?

It took a second overdose to end my life to realize that there was a Power who was greater than I was. God spoke to me when I woke up from my overdose and proclaimed I would not die and that He had plans for me to serve Him. It seems that I wasn't ready to accept God (and accept that I was an alcoholic) until that night.

It is said that you come to faith with God (or, the Higher Power of your choice) in one of two ways. The most common way is to spend years learning about God and then one day declaring your belief. The other way, which is rarer, is the way I came to find God (or He found me.) It was instantaneous, unexpected, and dramatic.

I've come to understand that Step Two gives me hope. Hope that someone greater than I am would be with me during my lifetime of recovery. Hope when I realized He forgave me my past sins. Hope that I could be a faithful follower of God. And hope that my soul was no longer condemned to hell.

Upon the completion of Step Two, I now had two tools in my toolbox with which to face the demons of my alcoholism— honesty and hope.

Step Three

Step Three- "Made a decision to turn our will and lives over to the care of God as we understood him."

"For God is working in you, giving you the desire and the power to do what pleases him." Philippians 2:13

Step Three means having a willingness and faith to trust your Higher Power. After I studied and worked Steps One and Two, how could I not have trust and faith in God? He was the Shepherd that brought me back to the flock of ninety-nine when I was lost. He saved me from the death of both of my over-doses. He demonstrates his love to me daily. I wake up thinking about God, talking with God during the day and going to bed praying to God.

I know that the day God spoke to me, I turned my life over to Him. I found God at the age of seventy-one and revel in his wisdom, protection, love, and forgiveness. Today, I can't imagine not giving my life to God, especially when He is such a part of my recovery and return to life.

I spent a lifetime not having faith and not trusting. I had learned as a child that if you trust, you get hurt. Was it any wonder that I felt betrayed, defensive, angry, fearful, and depressed? To cope with these feelings, my solution was to drink because then I didn't have to be honest about my fears.

My life has been totally different and rewarding since I admitted I was powerless over alcohol, that my life was unmanageable, that there was a Power greater than myself to help me overcome my alcoholism and I was willing to turn my life over to God.

Now I had honesty, hope and faith in my toolbox and was beginning to feel better about myself.

"Then he said to the crowd, if any of you wants to be my follower, you must turn from your selfish ways, take up your cross daily, and follow me." Luke 9:23

Step Four

Step Four- "Made a searching and fearless and moral inventory of ourselves."

"Let us examine our ways and test them, and let us return to the LORD." Lamentations 3:40

In Step Four, we are asked to do an inventory of our defects. This exercise helps us to begin to identify the causes of our drinking. These include thoughts, emotions and actions that have ruled our lives. As alcoholics, we justified our bad behavior and blamed other people, places, or things for the problems we had created.

This was, and still is, a difficult task for me to start and complete. After all, I felt I was perfect and someone else should take the blame for my behaviors. So, to start my list, I began in my childhood.

- I inherited my disease from my mother.
- I isolated myself because I didn't feel worthy of friends.
- I lived in fear that my parents wouldn't love me.
- I was never smart enough, pretty enough, or thin enough.
- I strived for perfectionism thinking it would bring me comfort.
- I began drinking at the early age of eight.

In an effort not to become totally overwhelmed, I looked at the list and tried to make sense of it before I went to my adolescent, teen, and older years.

- Geneticists believe that alcoholism tendency is inherited. What does the Serenity Prayer say? "God, give me the courage to accept the things I cannot change..." When I finally came to terms with this factor, it was easier to forgive my mother and her behaviors. And, yes, to forgive myself.

- I blamed my mother and her alcoholism for my lack of friends. I was ashamed when I had a schoolmate over to the house and mother was drinking and/or was drunk. I know now that she was programed to act the way she did. I don't know if sixty years ago, there was such shame around alcoholism that no one talked about it, or if there was no shame and we still didn't talk about alcoholism. It's true that I couldn't control my genetic pool but perhaps I may have been able to control when, where and how much I drank if I hadn't had too many personality defects.

- I longed for parental love and when I didn't get any, I became more and more perfectionistic and angry. I don't remember any hugs, kisses or my parents spending time with me growing up. I was so hungry for love and attention that I ran from my parents and home after graduating from high school and nursing school, seeking others who might love me. This was never going to work because I found what I thought was solace and love was in a bottle of booze.

- If I was loved as a child, I doubt I would have had feelings of not being smart enough, pretty enough, or thin enough. Lack of parental love during childhood, called neglect, has negative impacts on a person, especially early in life. As a result, individuals lack self-esteem and have difficulty with relationships. I felt so strongly about this concept that I wrote an article entitled, "Love Deprivation" for a national nursing magazine. The article included research and case studies. Of course, my story was one of the case studies.

- The harder I tried for perfectionism, the further I got from the feelings of being perfect. I maintained a nearly 4.0 GPA throughout my educational years, I sought strength to be the perfect daughter and I had a dream of becoming the perfect medical doctor. As much as I wanted feedback from my parents, it was lacking. When I completed the nurse practitioner program at the age of forty, my parents didn't congratulate me or acknowledge that I had an advanced degree. Rather than feeling accomplished, I was crushed.

- My early drinking became a personality defect as I grew older. At the age of eight, I didn't have the maturity and insight to know I was far too young to drink. What I did know was it gave me some time with my mother. She approved of the cocktails I drank. My negative feelings of not feeling loved or fitting in with my school friends lessened the more that I drank.

As I looked at my list, I began to realize how isolated, lonely, and miserable I had become. Although I definitely had what I thought was an exciting life, I experienced it alone.

After my first overdose, I began to examine how I lived my life with alcohol. As I drank, I became more isolated whether it be emotionally or physically. I shut myself off from the world. The next step, depression, was quick to set in and all of my defects became the monsters in my life.

When I retired, I started writing– fiction, non-fiction and poetry. In my poetry, I had an internal person called "My Dark Side." She was the one who talked me into feeling depressed, lonely, and suicidal. One day after I quit drinking, I had an "aha" moment and realized that My Dark Side was actually Satan who had invaded my body and soul.

Depression is a disease that is not easy to explain. It extends deep into my body and mind and is as physically painful as any illness I have ever experienced. I hurt to the core and at times I would find myself bent over with the pain and crying uncontrollably. From time to time, I would relinquish myself to hours of mental health therapy only to find it wasn't working for me. Was it that I was afraid of what therapy would unveil?

After depression were feelings of suicide. These feelings hurt as deeply as depression, with the exception that suicide is lethal and non-reversible. I experienced dying once with my first overdose and found leaving this earth was pleasant and comforting.

As I grew older, I learned to hide my alcohol. Who was I trying to kid? When you live with a spouse, there aren't many places you can hide a big bottle of booze that they can't inadvertently find. Nor was it easy to drink in solitude. Yet, I continued to look for secret cubby holes that would accommodate my stash and where I could drink without being found. Even when I was widowed a number of years later, I would hide my liquor thinking that if someone came to the house unexpectedly, they wouldn't see a bottle of half empty scotch on the kitchen counter at two in the afternoon.

The day I went to detox, I asked my friend to pour my alcohol stash down the drain. From my bedroom, I heard, "How much alcohol do you have?" I had to chuckle when I went out to the kitchen and began to reveal all of my hiding places.

For a meaningful relationship, trust and respect cannot be separated. I didn't feel worthy so I knew I couldn't trust anyone, and neither could I respect them and/or be respected. I was always trying to be and do better– those are impossible attributes to accomplish in a lifetime. And the all-time feeling of not being loved– how it has dominated my world.

My fourth tool in dealing with my alcoholism was courage. The courage to examine my life, the courage to admit my defects and the courage to begin to understand how they affected my life and living. Now I had honesty, faith, hope, and courage in my toolbox of sobriety.

Step Five

Step Five- "Admitted to God, to others and to another human being the exact nature of our wrongs."

I wondered just what Step Five entailed. Would I have to send out a bulletin telling the world about my alcoholism and defects? Was it sufficient to tell my close friends (of which, I have two) of my behaviors. Or would this be a process in which I revealed my addiction?

When I gave up alcohol and gave my life to God, things became more clear and easier to understand. I had a disease and as with any disease, there are symptoms to be dealt with. I wanted to get well and stay well from my alcoholism. The only way I could do this was to give my life to God, admit that I am an alcoholic, work the Twelve Steps and not be ashamed of who I am or how my disease has affected me. I began by being honest about my disease.

- I now used phrases like, "I don't drink".
- I am able to say, "I'm an alcoholic," without shame or guilt.
- I began to share my story of isolation, depression, drinking and suicidal thoughts in hopes that it may help others who are experiencing the same feelings.
- I removed all alcohol and alcohol related wine glasses, high ball glasses, cute napkins with quotes about alcohol, wine openers, etc. from my home.
- I was honest about my medical history and no longer listed my prior alcohol intake as any less than it was.
- I question the alcohol content in foods or beverages.

I found that by having the integrity to be honest and forthright, people accepted me for who I was, not what I had been and, for the most part, are extremely supportive of my recovery and values.

Integrity, the tool I've added in Step Five, is based on strong morals, and carrying these out in my daily life. I've found it easy to be honest with my story because without honesty and sharing, I know that I would be back in the throes of drinking.

My toolbox was beginning to fill up with wonderful qualities I was learning to incorporate into my new life of recovery– honesty, hope, faith, courage, and integrity.

Step Six

Step Six- "We were entirely ready to have God remove all of these defects."

Why would I want to hang onto the character defects I identified in Step Four? I was, admittedly, lonely, and unhappy. And I was killing myself with a lifetime of drinking. Why wouldn't I have these defects removed by God?

The key to Step Six is the willingness to share our defects with God and others. As I attended more AA meetings, I began to understand the importance of members sharing their stories with the group. I also realized it was important in my recovery to share my story. Although I become tired reciting my history of alcoholism, each time I learned something new about myself.

God knows our defects. How difficult is it to ask him to remove them from our lives? This is the power of prayer. God wants us to ask for redemption from our disease and its associated defects. All we need is a willingness to rid ourselves of our defects and the courage to ask God to remove them.

At the end of Step Six, I was halfway through the Twelve Steps. I had honestly admitted I was powerless over alcohol. I found hope that I could be restored to sanity by God. I learned that through faith, I was able to turn my life over to God. I had courageously made an inventory of my defects. I had the integrity to admit to God, myself, and others the nature of my defects. And I was willing to ask God to remove my defects.

The beauty and workability of the Twelve Steps was that they were beginning to make sense in a way I could use them in my daily life. I was ready to move onto Step Seven.

"Humble yourselves before the Lord, and he will lift you up in honor." James 4:10

Step Seven

Step Seven- "Humbly asked Him to remove our shortcomings."

Now that I had admitted I had defects or shortcomings, I was ready and willing to ask God to remove these from my person and soul.

I had a lot of defects to deal with and they all ultimately ended up in a desire to take my life and leave this earth on a permanent basis. I was too emotionally and physically sick to take into consideration this was a lethal solution to my "now" problem. Did I understand that I could never come back from death?

When I found faith in God and the love He unconditionally gives us, I found a new meaning to life and a reason to go on living. That nearly fatal night when I swallowed too many pills and drank too much scotch was the last time I felt like I wanted to die. In sobriety, I've found God is the reason I'm still alive and the reason I want to continue to live and live a life with God.

By humbly asking God to remove my shortcomings, I have been given a new and meaningful life, one that I am not willing to cast aside with alcohol. Humility was added to my toolbox.

I was becoming more comfortable with my new life of sobriety. That was until I read Step Eight and Nine.

Step Eight took some thinking and making a list was going to be difficult. However, I approached this step as I did my recovery– one step at a time.

"But if we confess our sins to him, he is faithful and just to forgive us our sins and to cleanse us from all wickedness." 1 John 1:9

Step Eight

Step Eight- "Made a list of persons we had harmed and became willing to make amends to them."

I found I could put those I had harmed into three categories:

- *My Parents–* Unfortunately, by the time I got into recovery, both of my parents were deceased. I did, however, talk with them posthumously and talked about my feelings growing up, their dysfunctional parenting, the defects I acquired throughout my life and that I forgave them and myself for the tormented childhood I had.

- *My Siblings–* About six months after I returned home from my rehabilitation program, I wrote a letter to my three siblings. In this letter, I outlined my alcoholism, recovery, and desire to reconnect with my two brothers and sister. I had a positive response from one of my brothers and my sister. The second brother only said that I gave him a lot to think about. When I didn't hear back, I attempted to contact him two more times and to get together with him. To date, this has not been accomplished. I can't control my brother's emotions or feelings, but I can get on with my life.

- *My Husbands–* I divorced my first husband and have not been successful in locating him. So, I talked to him in my thoughts about our marriage, our drinking, and our mistrust of one another. I hoped that he was able to receive my thought message.

- My second husband has been deceased since 2011. Since his death, I have written him letters, wrote poetry to him and thought about the dysfunction we had before he died. Doing this has helped me feel better about not being able to help him during his dying days.

As for others, there aren't many who are still alive, or I know of their whereabouts. If I could contact them, then I did and usually got a response like, "I didn't know there was a problem."

In Step Eight I had acquired *compassion* to put in my toolbox and was ready to proceed with Step Nine.

Do to others as you would like them to do to you." Luke 6:31

Step Nine

"Made direct amends to such people whenever possible, except when to do so would injure them or others."

I decided that making amends to people I had harmed would fall into three categories:

- *Category One*– those that I could approach immediately as long as I was maintaining my sobriety. This was easy because these individuals were currently in my life.

- *Category Two*– those individuals with whom I could make partial retribution lest full amends would be harmful to them or associated people.

- *Category Three*– those whom I would not be able to make amends with.

- My toolbox was getting close to being full as I added justice to my other recovery tools.

> *"So if you are presenting a sacrifice at the altar in the Temple and you suddenly remember that someone has something against you, leave your sacrifice there at the altar. Go and be reconciled to that person. Then come and offer your sacrifice to God." Matthew 5: 23-24*

Step Ten

"Continued to take personal inventory and when we were wrong, promptly admitted it."

Step Ten can be considered a maintenance step as we continually review our list of personal defects and make amends to those we have harmed.

Perseverance is the key to Step Ten and is meant to be practiced daily as we review our defects and the progress, we've made to correct them.

Once we become comfortable with our Twelve Step program, it can be easy to gloss over Step Ten thinking we have already made our inventory list. What becomes exciting and essential to my recovery is to journal my accomplishments, add my success stories and how I have worked on, or abated, my defects.

> *"Because of the privilege and authority God has given me, I give you this warning: Don't think you are better than you really are. Be honest in your evaluation of yourselves, measuring yourselves by the faith God has given us." Romans 12:3*

Step Eleven

"Sought through prayer and meditation to improve our conscious contact with God as we understood Him, praying only for knowledge of His will for us and the power to carry that out."

Try as I might, I was never able to get the knack of meditation during my four-week rehabilitation stay. Getting my mind to go blank, just wasn't happening. One day, I was reading about the many ways one can meditate and I felt liberated. These are a few of my new meditative techniques.

- Being in nature and observing the wonders of the earth God made for us.
- Sitting outside watching the sunset or sunrise.
- Soaking in a warm bath with the glow of candles around me and reviewing how good God has been in my recovery.
- Attending church and participating in the worship songs. At first, I was timid and my voice was small. Now, I sing with my entire heart and a full voice. How I love to feel the Holy Spirit during worship.
- Engaging in prayer is a perfect way for me to meditate and be in contact with God. I pray to God as if he were my best friend, as He is, and share my day, thoughts, recovery progress and any temptations that Satan has given me that day.

"May the words of my mouth and the meditation of my heart be pleasing to you, O Lord, my rock and my redeemer?" Psalm 19:14

Step Twelve

"Having had a spiritual awakening as the result of these steps, we tried to carry this message to alcoholics, and to practice these principles in our lives.

Recovery is a process of giving and taking– by giving it away, we get to keep it. Step Twelve, *service*, states that we should seek opportunities to support the principles of Alcoholics Anonymous.

Service can be accomplished by living the principles of the Twelve Steps and proclaiming them to the AA community, assisting with meetings and having one-on-one interactions with a person.

> *"Dear brothers and sisters, if another believer is overcome by some sin, you who are godly should gently and humbly help that person back onto the right path. And be careful not to fall into the same temptation yourself." Galatians 6:1*

The Twelve Principles of Alcoholics Anonymous Principles of Recovery for My Toolbox

---

The Twelve Steps are based on principles, solid truths or qualities that are essential to our recovery. Living by these principles changes lives radically, leading us from isolation and despair of addiction to the freedom of recovery.

Honesty

Hope

Faith

Courage

Integrity

Willingness

Humility

Compassion

Justice

Perseverance

Spiritual Awareness

Service

Recovery Worksheets

Recovery requires time, commitment, retrospection, communication, discussion, review and redirection to keep you on the right path toward sobriety. I've found that initiating and maintaining written records helps to show you your progress and how you can improve.

The enclosed recovery sheets are included to assist a person in recovery to steps are not forgotten or short sided. The Alcoholic Anonymous Twelve Step Program requires that all steps are completed and done so in a systematic and sequential manner.

Recovery Worksheet#1
- Keeping a Journal

A journal is paramount to recovery. There is a saying that "It isn't true until it is said." The same is true of recovery, "It doesn't happen unless it's written down." Use a notebook or computer to jot down notes and thoughts as you begin, or continue, your recovery journey.

- List what you think your problems are.

- As you review these problems, notice what secrets are associated with them.

- What excuses do you use for your problems (addictive behaviors?)

Recovery Worksheet#2 – Identifying Problems

We all have problems; however, the addict's mind processes these situations and responds differently to them than the non-addict. What problems you have experienced in your life as an alcoholic?

Recovery Worksheet#3
—What are Your Secrets?

Addicts have a significant number of secrets and the secrets themselves are a problem. Secrets are kept from spouses, children, parents, friends, co-workers, and others in your life. For each secret you are keeping, you are hiding a part of you. Think about your secrets and list them below.

Recovery Worksheet#4
–Excuses for Your Behavior

Addicts create rationales for their behaviors, and these are usually in terms of justification ("I need a drink to loosen up.") List the excuses you have typically used for your behavior (i.e. "it's five o'clock somewhere".)

Recovery Worksheet#5 – Draw Your Addictive Cycle

Every addict engages in a relationship (alcohol, drugs) that produces a desired mood change or state of intoxication. Use the space below to map out your addictive cycle– those events that result in undesirable behaviors. For instance, my addictive cycle is drawn below,

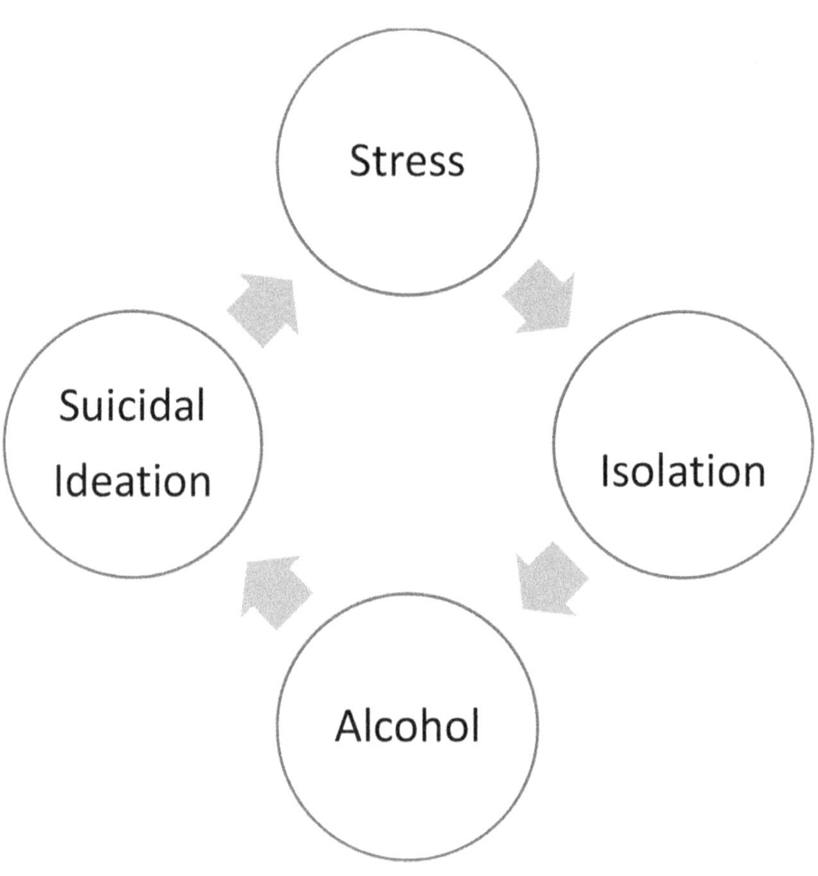

Recovery Worksheet#6
–Your Recovery Goals

Journaling your recovery goals are helpful to keep you on target during your recovery time. Consider how you are going to conduct your life to remain sober and list them below.

Recovery Worksheet#7
– The Start of Your Addiction

Thinking back to your childhood, what were the events that were the start of your addiction? At what age do you believe addiction was part of who your are now? At what age was your addiction at its highest? Was there a specific time in your life when you had no control over your addiction?

Recovery Worksheet#8
–A Powerless Inventory

List as many examples of the times you were powerless to stop using your addictive substance. What were the consequences of your powerlessness.

Recovery Worksheet#9
– An Unmanageability Inventory

Unmanageability means your addiction created chaos and damage in your life. List as many examples as you can to show your life has become unmanageable.

Recovery Worksheet#10 – The Reasons I Love Me

In closing, write something good about yourself.

RESOURCES

No one is ever too broken, Too scared,
Or too far gone to create change.
Never stop fighting.
Never lose faith.

https://www.alcoholrehabguide.org/alcohol/causes

Carnes, Patrick. *A Gentle Path through the Twelve Steps: A Classic Guide for all People in the Process of Recovery.* Hazelden Press. Center City, Minnesota, 2012.

Carnes P. Ph.D., Carnes, S. Ph.D. and Bailey, John, M.D. *Facing Addiction: Starting Recovery from Alcohol and Drugs.* Gentle Path Press. Scottsdale, Arizona, 2001.

Carson, Rick. Taming Your Gremlin: *A Surprisingly Simple Method for Getting Out of Your Own Way.* William Morrow, New York, New York. 2003.

Centers for Disease Control and Prevention. Alcohol Use and Your Health. January 14, 2021. https://www.cdc.gov/alcohol/fact-sheets/alcohol-use.htm

Covington, Stephanie S. A Woman's Way through the Twelve Steps. Hazelden Publishing, Center City, Minnesota, 1994.

Harvard Health Publishing. Sorting out the health effects of alcohol. August 6, 2018. https://www.health.harvard.edu/blog/sorting-out-the-health-effects-of-alcohol-2018080614427

Genetics and alcoholism. Genetics and alcoholism. May 28, 2013. https://www.ncbi.nlm.nih.gov/pmc/articles/PMC4056340/

Iliff, Brenda. A Woman's Guide to Recovery. Hazelden. Center City, Minnesota, 2008.

Ingram, Chip. *God as He Longs You to See Him*. Baker Books. Grand Rapids, Michigan, 2004.

Mellody, Pia. *Facing Co-Dependence: What It Is, Where It Comes From, How It Sabotages Our Lives*. Harper One. New York, New York. 2003.

Mental and Emotional Effects of Alcoholism. Addictionintervention.com

National Institute on Alcohol Abuse and Alcoholism. Alcohol's Effects on the Body. https://www.niaaa.nih.gov/alcohols-effects-health/alcohols-effects-body

National Institute on Alcohol Abuse and Alcoholism. Genetics of Alcohol Use Disorder. Number 4,2008. https://www.niaaa.nih.gov/alcohols-effects-health/alcohol-use-disorder/genetics-alcohol-use-disorder

Northwestern Medicine. How Alcohol Impacts the Brain. https://www.nm.org/healthbeat/healthy-tips/alcohol-and-the-brain

Prin, John Howard. *Secret Keeping: Overcoming Hidden Habits and Addictions*. New World Library. Novato, California, 2006.

The Life Recovery Bible. Carol Stream, Illinois, Tyndale House Publishers. 2015.

Twelve Steps and Twelve Traditions. Alcoholics Anonymous World Services, Inc. New York, New York, 1952, 1953 and 1981.

Rehabs.com. An Americanaddictioncenters Resource.

Twerski, Abraham, M.D. *Addictive Thinking: Understanding Self-Deception*. Hazelden Publishing. Center City, Minnesota, 1997.

www.altamirarecovery.com

Young, Sarah. *Jesus Calling*. Thomas Nelson. China, 2001.

CHAPTER TEN

The Butterfly Sings Recovery Poetry

We all know that butterflies can't talk or sing. So, why did I choose this spectacular insect for my butterfly poems? The butterfly reminds me of the journey I have been on and my love for and devotion to God.

These magnificent butterflies have a life span of twenty-eight days. In this very short time, they transform through four stages from an egg, a caterpillar, a cocoon and finally a beautiful butterfly.

I have also experienced four stages in my life. In my first stage of believing and faith, I was a non-believer for the first seventy-one years of my life. I was also an alcoholic during most of these years. One night in May 2018, my second stage, God came to me and told me he had plans for me to serve him. I spent many long hours studying the bible, in fellowship with other Christians and reading the word of God. It was during this third stage, that I began to understand God and his love for me and his forgiveness of my sins. The beauty of the first three stages on my journey was that they prepared for my fourth stage, to serve God and spread his word to others.

So, you see, God created both the butterfly and me and gave us both beautiful attributes in which to reach others. The butterfly with her beautiful wings and flight. Me with my new faith and spreading His word; and, my recovery.

I hope that you enjoy reading my stories and I ask that you pray for me as I continue my voyage.

Sandy

A Letter from Sobriety

Hello, this is your new butterfly friend Sobriety,
We met five years ago when you were high on anxiety.
You were drinking from dawn to bedtime just to get through the day,
Your life was dark, dismal, unproductive and no longer gay.

I've watched your downward progress from the skies above,
I knew deep inside there was someone who was looking for love.
You once loved deeply, and death took that away.
You resorted to alcohol to hide you sorrows and felt betrayed.

One night you finally hit the bottom of your dreams,
You had pondered death and different schemes.
But God had an alternate plan for you and your life,
You were to live and throw away your miserable strife.

I was ready to meet you as I had waited for a lifetime,
You poured out the alcohol that was your friend for a long time.
We both went to detox where your body began to cleanse,
We began a journey of faith and love as new friends.

I've watched your mind and body change and grow,
You've learned about happiness, peace, and joy with a radiant glow.
I know we will always be friends and share a connection,
For I am here by your side with love, guidance, and protection.

A Transformed Life

Addiction changes who you are and how you think,
You find the world becomes a puzzle of confusion in a wink.
One day you find a new friend named Recovery,
You become wiser and stronger in your discovery.

With Recovery you learn to laugh and be gay,
The world is no longer shades of gray.
You learn more about your addiction,
Shame and guilt become past afflictions.

You own your story by telling it to others,
It's one of your new life wonders.
You found different friends and hobbies,
They were sober, fun, and not naughty.

You needed to cry and found the tears,
Tears of unwantedness over the years.
You wanted to live to face another day,
You soon found the courage to stay.

You are not the person you were,
You fought to be become your new her.
Your old life is gone forever,
Now you have God and love together.

The Girl with Wings of Hope

Once upon a time very long ago in days gone by,
There was a young girl who knew how to fly.
She would fly around her world,
Seeking wonders as they unfurled.

The young girl was a happy and joyous child,
There was nothing in her world she saw defiled.
Then entered the prince of darkness,
His powers were great and seemed harmless.

I bring you a new enticing beverage to drink,
You will be able to fly higher and brighter in a wink.
The prince of darkness smiled with devious deceit,
Giving the young girl the drink so cold and sweet.

The young girl took a small drink and smiled,
Goodness this is so yummy she said feeling wild.
The prince of darkness knew he had captured her,
He gave her more until she spoke in a slur.

My wings won't move, and I feel dizzy,
My head feels like it's all in a tizzy.
Then my dear you must drink more,
Give me your glass and I'll gladly pour.

What do they call this confusing concoction?
It seems to be a toxin is there another option?
You drank alcohol that's known the world around,
There is no other that affects you so profound.

The young girl drank more of the alcohol,
Until her head swam and she felt like a rag doll.
She drank more and more for many years,
When she couldn't stop, she wept tears.

One day when she was a teenager and unhappy,
She decided she was tired of feeling sad and crappie.

The prince of darkness showed up one day,
Come with me and forever be gay.

Knowing this was not the way she wanted to die,
She dusted off her wings and attempted to fly,
You will never fly while you have intoxicated wings,
Your wings are limp and fragile as wet strings.

The teenager too soon became a woman,
The alcohol had made her feel less than human.
How can I get out of this debauchery I'm in?
I must shun the prince of darkness and his gin.

The troubled woman prayed each day for guidance,
Her prayers were sincere as she talked to God in silence.
Please rid me of the prince of darkness and his evil drink,
I feel so lost and sad that I want to fall into a brink.

God came to the troubled woman one glorious night,
Believe in me and I will help you make everything right.
The alcohol has made you sad with shame and guilt,
Your life has been like a twisted and ugly quilt.

God said if you want joy and happiness do not drink,
Cast aside the prince of darkness and his wicked stink,
Admit that you are powerless over alcohol and booze,
Believe that I am your Higher Power for you to use.

The curious woman turned her life over to God,
She found with God she wasn't so much at odds.
There are eleven more actions for you to take,
For this side of sobriety in you still awaits.

What are these actions I must practice?
What would be their steps of exactness?
This is what you must do said God,
Follow each step to drop your drunken façade.

The thankful woman did an inventory of herself,

She admitted her wrongs to God and other selves.
She told God she was ready to remove her defects,
And asked God to humbly take away these effects.

A list was made of all she had done wrong,
Making amends to those as she went along.
As time went on, she again reviewed her wrongs,
And praised God with thanks and her amazing songs.

She prayed and meditated asking for God's guidance,
To others she took these steps and actions of compliance.
The woman who was plagued by the prince of darkness,
Learned that his beverage was not harmless.

Today the sober woman loves her reawakened life,
She has found a sobriety organization and has a new drive.
Finding God and the steps to maintain her sobriety,
Have given the woman strength to re-enter society.

With a clear mind and an open heart, she decrees,
You can be happy and sober in steps of degrees.
Love God and your neighbor and share your story,
There is someone out there who also wants glory.

The sober woman with her dusted wings,
Flew high into the clouds as confident as kings.
She will return again soon for many have strayed,
She will help those addicts who have hoped and prayed.

The Lioness and the Butterfly

Once upon a time in the land of uncertainty,
There was a timid lioness who lived carelessly.
She was a pretty lioness all dressed in fur,
But inside she was afraid of life and her interior.

She would wander around the land lonely and roar,
Her lion friends thought she was an absolute bore.
How do I become one of those confident lions?
I want to be strong, courageous, and reliant.

One day she ran into a little butterfly on a log,
The butterfly sat and sat as though in a fog.
Aren't you afraid of me the lioness asked?
Why should I be the butterfly answered steadfast?

Because I am the most ferocious animal in the forest,
And you my dear butterfly are most certainly the smallest.
Size makes no difference it's what's inside that counts,
And with that the butterfly came closer in a pounce.

I'd like to be known as a courageous lioness,
To be magnificent and rid myself of this shyness.
Courage isn't being bolder than the rest,
It's not feeling you are better than the best.

Courage is the ability to be strong and persevere,
When life seems difficult and severe.
True courage is facing danger when you're afraid,
Courage is knowing when you've strayed.

The lioness thought about what the butterfly said,
I've been withdrawn and didn't care what was ahead.
Stay with me little butterfly and help me learn who I am,
Be my guide and support as I learn my courage program.

The lioness learned how to be courageous in the forest,
She no longer needed to roar in fear and was now honest.
Her courage grew with the little butterfly as her sponsor,
Today the lioness is courageous and lives by her honor.

The Healing Butterfly

Do you see the beautiful butterfly flying over your head?
She is sprinkling you with magical dust as you look at what's ahead.
She has butterfly dust to help you during recovery to get well,
All you have to do is ask her and she will sit for a spell.

You and the magical butterfly snuggled together,
Breathing and dreaming settled in light as a feather.
Waking you asked where is that butterfly when I need her?
The butterfly was sleeping beside you with her soft purrs.

Suddenly there was a flash of color spinning,
Is that you little butterfly you asked grinning?
The magical butterfly had lots of recovery get-well glitter,
She flew and landed on you in such a flitter.

You have been so quiet I didn't know you needed me,
I will stay with you until you are well she did decree.
Relieved you shut your eyes and went to sleep,
The magical butterfly slept while you counted sheep.

When you awoke you were feeling better,
You wondered if you needed your butterfly sitter.
The butterfly refused to leave saying she would stay,
Declaring she was happy and would never stray.

As the story goes you became best pals.
Yours is a story of recovery, magic, and butterfly gals.

The Love Butterfly

It was a beautiful warm and sunny day,
The butterfly was flying about looking for play.
I wonder if I can find a sweet innocent girl,
To surprise and land on her in a twirl?

The butterfly flew up high in the sky,
She loved flying with her wings held high.
She was a dramatically colored butterfly,
Showing her purple colors to all nearby.

She was enjoying her peaceful day of play,
When she heard a sound that gave her dismay.
It sounded like someone was unhappy and crying,
The wails were so captivating as to be dying.

The butterfly flew rapidly toward the sobbing,
She flew so fast her heart was throbbing.
Soon she spied a young girl beside a brook,
She slowed her speed to take a better look.

The young lass was curled up in a ball,
She was hiding her sobs and not standing tall.
The butterfly landed on her shoulder,
Confused the butterfly grew bolder.

Excuse me lass the butterfly said quietly,
Are you going to sniffle and cry endlessly?
The young lass looked up with a start,
Who is that talking and scaring my heart?

'Tis only me the butterfly replied,
I didn't mean to take you for a frightful ride.
I heard you crying and wanted to help,
You sound like a young pup trying to yelp.

Is that a butterfly talking to me?
The butterfly said that's who it would be.

I asked you if I could help with your quandary.
Can you really help me the lass replied fondly?

Absolutely, but first I must know what's wrong,
Can you dry your tears and give me a song?
What should I sing about the lass wondered?
What is so terrible as to make you plunder?
The lass knew she wanted help but from a butterfly.
Okay she thought there is nothing else for me to try.
She dried her tears and gave a big sigh,
The butterfly sat waiting in the by and by.

I'm lonely and sad because no one loves me,
I have no joy in my life even though I plea.
My self-esteem is as low as a bug,
I can't remember when I had a hug.

Do you love yourself the butterfly inquired?
I don't know but love is what I desire.
The more you love yourself the more love you receive,
Self-love will take away what you grieve.

Loving yourself starts with liking yourself,
Which starts with respecting yourself,
Which starts with powerful thinking about yourself.
Before you can test love on others you must love yourself.

Do you mean that if I like and love myself I can be joyful?
If you are sincere about yourself you will also be playful.
The lass stood up dried her tears and kissed the butterfly,
Just then the butterfly flew high into the sky,

Magical purple butterflies do exist,
You only need to listen closely and persist.
Once you experience a magical purple butterfly,
Your heart will know their magic in the by and by.

The Courageous Butterfly

The butterfly, what a courageous creature,
A creature that crawls the earth,
And ultimately flies the skies.

As a caterpillar it exposes itself to danger,
Close to the ground it is prey,
Does it know the perils it faces?

It subsists on the plant it was born on,
Eating its way to maturity,
It now creates a safe home, the pupa.

When the pupa is ready to split open,
A butterfly emerges and waits,
Courageously for its wings to dry.

Now the butterfly is a courageous creature,
And is ready for flight,
Knowing it will only live two weeks.

Dutifully the butterfly mates,
The males die after mating,
The females die after laying eggs.

In a short-time span,
The butterfly faces danger,
Providing food for other creatures.

Does it know the jeopardy of its life?
Does it know the curiosity of being a caterpillar?
Does it know the pleasure its wings and beauty bring?

Have you thought about the similarities?
Of the life of a butterfly and your life?
The courage you both have facing life?

As infants, humans are dependent upon a food supply,
As humans we grow through stages of growth,

We live in our pupa until we reach maturity.

Maturity brings us the beauty of life,
We are courageous, faithful, and loving,
Our beauty is only magnified by our love of God.

We fly to heights unknown with our faith,
We bring joy to others with our inner beauty,
And we die having left our heritage.

God knew what he was doing with his creations,
The creation of the butterfly and the human.
He instilled us with courage to face life.

Butterflies are magical,
Humans are children of God,
Both are courageous,
Both are beautiful and endearing.

When the Butterfly Sings

When butterflies fly their wings sing,
What pleasure and beauty their music brings?
You must listen carefully and dutifully,
To hear their songs fill the air wonderfully.

Butterflies remind us of the beauty God gives us,
Their beautiful colors and elusive patterns of blush.
They seem to have some mesmerizing powers,
Because we can hear their songs for hours.

When we are happy butterflies flutter around,
When we are sad butterflies sit on the ground.
When we laugh butterflies twirl and swirl,
When we cry the butterfly's song is shrill.

When a butterfly sits on your shoulder,
It is confident, aware and bolder.
That's when you can hear her sounds the best,
She sings her butterfly songs softly at rest.

The next time you see a butterfly in the air,
Sing a merry tune with her without a care,
For the butterfly is like God,
She hears you best when you speak aloud.

The Girl and Her Butterfly

Little butterfly where are you?
I need to find you what can I do?
My darling girl you need to believe,
It does no good to be sad and grieve.

You are so right my sweet butterfly,
I do believe you are here she sighed.
Won't you fly over and sit with me?
How about under that shady tree?

The girl and the butterfly sat under the shady tree,
Now what is it you needed to see me about my sweet?
I want to talk about life the girl smiled and said,
Hmm, that's a heavy topic for such a beautiful day.

I know but it's been on my mind and I want to talk,
Do you ever wonder how long you will live by the clock?
My dear my life is very short as I fly the skies,
I was a caterpillar and now I'm a beautiful butterfly.

Life seems to be ever so long as I grow older,
I don't know how many years I'll live and be bolder.
My darling it's not how long you live but how you live,
Only God knows how long you will be on earth to give.

Beautiful butterfly explain to me about giving,
God gives you the gift of the Holy Spirit and loving.
The Holy Spirit lives within you and teaches virtue,
Among them are peace, humility, and love to nurture.

As a child of God all you need to do is believe,
Lead a God-like life and worship God and receive.
Receive God's love and forgiveness as a child of God,
Honor Him and spend your life with God being awed.

God loves you unconditionally and will never leave you,
Regardless of your sins He will always forgive you.

He wants to hear from you in prayer throughout the day,
God loves to hear you speak aloud as you pray.

The day you die should make no difference to you,
If you live according to the plan God's set for you,
There will be a place in heaven for you,
God loves you and is only waiting for you.

Dear butterfly with your gorgeous purple wings,
I will miss you with what your inspirations bring,
I will live according to God's plans and designs,
Living each day to its fullest as my faith realigns.

The butterfly flew away for the last time,
For you see her lifespan was in overtime.
She had fulfilled her mission with society,
The girl began a new life of God, faith and sobriety.

AN ENDING AND A BEGINNING

A spiritual gift is given to each of us so we can help each other. To one person the Spirit gives the ability to give wise advice; to another the same Spirit gives a gift of special knowledge. The same Spirit gives great faith to another, and to someone else the one Spirit gives the gift of healing. He gives one person the power to perform miracles and another the ability to prophesy. 1 Corinthians 12:7-10

This is my story. It's one of a life of drinking, solitude and isolation, depression and suicidal tendencies. I was fortunate that my habits and behaviors didn't get me in trouble. I never missed work because of drinking, I put myself through school to obtain a nursing undergraduate degree and a nurse practitioner graduate degree. Even though I drank, I advanced my career to the management level and became an adjunct professor at two universities. I spent ten years on the executive board of a national nursing organization attaining the position of executive president. I became certified as a personal trainer and incorporated wellness and fitness into my nurse practitioner practice. When I retired, I began writing fiction and non-fiction stories and have had my books published. I also discovered that I could play the piano after fifty years of abstinence.

Along the way of these accomplishments, my drinking increased, my life became more isolated and I became more depressed. I have always had difficulty with establishing and maintaining relationships. Now that I am sober, I realize my introversion was the result of wanting to stay home and drink in the privacy of my environment. This was compounded by feelings of inadequacy in groups and not feeling good enough about myself to be with others. This is all crazy because I'm intelligent, educated, talented and a helpful and caring individual. However, alcohol changes the way we feel about ourselves and the way we conduct our lives.

After more than six decades of drinking, I found God and sobriety. Learning to love myself and attain sobriety came with the potential price of nearly losing my life twice with attempted overdoses. Alcohol takes away one's feeling of self-love and love of others, it robs us of self-esteem and it destroys our bodies. Admitting myself to an alcohol rehabilitation program was the bravest thing I did in my life. I was giving up my way of living, the friendship I had with alcohol and losing my drinking buddies.

If I had not found God at the end of my drinking career, I'm not sure I would be sober today or alive or could have maintained a sober life. I'm a strong person and a survivor of my past, however, this may not have been enough to sustain my sobriety. My rehabilitation program was frustrating, and I fought it for four weeks. When I got out of the in-patient program, I knew it was up to me to maintain sobriety. I now had control of my life. I began to know God, became a Christian and was baptized.

God, Christianity and sobriety are the main focus of my life and living today. Each day, I thank God for my sobriety. I abstain from functions where alcohol is involved. I pray, meditate, study the bible, and facilitate bible study groups. I socialize with other recovering alcoholics and Christians and worship God each Sunday during church services. I seize every opportunity to talk with those users who are looking for guidance and sobriety. With the Holy Spirit residing within me, I feel at peace with life, my swearing has been abated, I look for the good in people and discourage gossip or talking ill of others.

God has gifted each of us in some way. We all have talents and special abilities. When we put ourselves down, we are rejecting these gifts from God rather than delighting in them. We don't need to build up our self-esteem, we just need to see more accurately who we are and how God has gifted us. Being in recovery is a unique gift in itself. We have suffered through the process of failure and deliverance. We are uniquely gifted to help others in similar ways. By sharing what God has done for us, we may be giving the gift of life to someone else in need.

I've shared my story and journey along the way to recovery and my new faith in God because I want others to know that they are not alone. There is always a person willing and wanting to help.

As recovering alcoholics, we learn to live for today. Yesterday is gone, as are the days of drinking. Today is today and the only day we can control. Tomorrow hasn't come yet, but can be filled with our dreams and hopes– a lifetime of sobriety.

My life of drinking is not something I'm proud of. What I'm proud of is that I had the strength, courage, fortitude, and commitment to give up the bottle, get my life together and, in the process, give my life to God and become a faithful Christian. God rescued me so that I could serve him now and in the afterlife.

God loves us and wants to help us. All we have to do is ask Him. With the help of God, our souls are being readied for a life of eternity with Him.

Thank you for reading my story and I hope it was helpful whether you are fighting alcoholism, drug addiction or have family members or friends you are concerned about. My thinking is clear, and I can engage in intellectual conversations and hobbies. Others who are alcohol dependent are not so lucky.

I praise God for looking after me the years of my drinking, coming to my rescue and saving my soul for an eternal life with Him.

Sandra Bobbitt
August 2023

ABOUT THE AUTHOR

Sandra L. Bobbitt

Sandy Bobbitt is a recovering alcoholic and resides in Wickenburg, Arizona with two cats. She spent her career helping others as a nurse practitioner, university professor and personal trainer. Now, in her retirement, she spends time helping others as a facilitator of bible studies, through the Twelve Step program, writing self-help books and articles and through her music.

After over sixty years of drinking, she hit rock bottom. She had no friends, no resources, had become isolated, depressed, and harbored suicidal thoughts. Knowing that she was an alcoholic, but in complete denial, she admitted herself to a drug and alcohol rehabilitation clinic.

Today, Sandy experiences the joy of God in her life, sobriety, and ongoing recovery. She wrote her story in hopes that it would help others who are addicts and may or may have not hit bottom. "If I can touch only one person, my life and writings will be meaningful."

Sandy can be reached at sandybobbitt@gmail.com